"We've got to do this fast,"

Luke said, unbuttoning his shirt.

"W-what are you doing . . . ?" Jenny asked, wide-eyed.

"Taking off my shirt." He tossed it on a chair, and she saw the wide bandage he'd attempted to wind around his torso. "I couldn't get this tight enough."

"You expect *me* to do it?" she asked in disbelief. "I think you'd better wait until your grandmother comes back."

"I don't want Stella to know. Now come on."

He watched, amused, as she hesitated, then approached him cautiously.

"Youch!" he exclaimed when her fingers touched his warm flesh. "Your hands are like ice!"

"Then I'll try hard not to touch you."

"Touch me all you want. I won't mind."

She glared up at him. "Do you want me to help you or not?"

"Okay, I'll be good." He smiled broadly. "And when I'm good, I'm very, very good. . . ."

Dear Reader,

Welcome to Silhouette—experience the magic of the wonderful world where two people fall in love. Meet heroines that will make you cheer for their happiness, and heroes (be they the boy next door or a handsome, mysterious stranger) who will win your heart. Silhouette Romance reflects the magic of love—sweeping you away with books that will make you laugh and cry, heartwarming, poignant stories that will move you time and time again.

In the coming months we're publishing romances by many of your all-time favorites, such as Diana Palmer, Brittany Young, Sondra Stanford and Annette Broadrick. Your response to these authors and our other Silhouette Romance authors has served as a touchstone for us, and we're pleased to bring you more books with Silhouette's distinctive medley of charm, wit and—above all—*romance*.

I hope you enjoy this book and the many stories to come. Experience the magic!

Sincerely,

Tara Hughes
Senior Editor
Silhouette Books

THERESA WEIR

Loving
Jenny

Silhouette *Romance*

Published by Silhouette Books New York

America's Publisher of Contemporary Romance

For Martha
who loves all creatures great and small

SILHOUETTE BOOKS
300 E. 42nd St., New York, N.Y. 10017

ISBN: 0-373-08650-4

First Silhouette Books printing May 1989

Printed in the U.S.A.

Books by Theresa Weir

Silhouette Romance

The Forever Man #576
Loving Jenny #650

THERESA WEIR

was born in Burlington, Iowa, and has lived in many different parts of the United States. Currently she resides in an Illinois community "so rural that there's only one traffic light in the entire county." She and her husband keep busy raising cattle, sheep and Australian shepherds, as well as their two children.

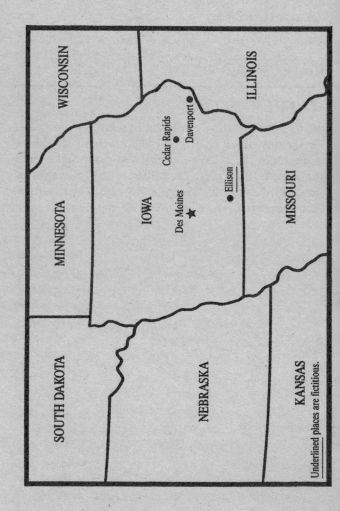

SOUTH DAKOTA

MINNESOTA

WISCONSIN

NEBRASKA

IOWA

Des Moines ★

Cedar Rapids ●

Davenport ●

Ellison ●

ILLINOIS

KANSAS

MISSOURI

Underlined places are fictitious.

Chapter One

Lucas Tate veered his '72 Chevy truck off the highway and sped toward the concrete block gas station.

The sixteen-hour days at his veterinary practice
combined with worry about what his eccentric grandmother would do next were pushing him to the limit,
both mentally and physically.

The station bell gave two feeble protests as his
truck's bald tires rolled over the worn-out hose and a
cloud of pulverized gravel caught up with him as he
braked to a jerking halt. Dust drifted in the open window, settling on his shaggy brown hair, making his
navy blue T-shirt and denim jeans look even more
faded than usual.

He inhaled, feeling fine dirt particles abrade his
lungs. A lot of good it had done to quit smoking, he

thought ruefully. Maybe the government should conduct a few tests on the passive inhalation of midwestern backroads.

He reached out the open window to grope along a door made sizzling hot by a relentless July sun. His long fingers made contact with the chrome handle, and he pushed in the button as he shoved one broad shoulder against the door. It opened grudgingly, dry hinges groaning in protest. But at least it opened. The door on the passenger side didn't work at all.

He'd thought about having it fixed once—the winter the latch had frozen and he'd been forced to crawl out the window right under Widow Simmons's disapproving glare. He'd muttered some self-conscious remark about the negative effects of below zero weather, only to have her respond by loftily informing him that the county veterinary service had certainly changed since Dr. Kiley's day.

He had been sorely tempted to tell her the truth: that her revered and now deceased Dr. Kiley had kept the local rendering works thriving. Luke had taken great satisfaction when, just a year after setting up his own practice, the carcass collectors had been forced to move to a more lucrative area. But Luke had been taught to respect his elders, and even at age thirty-two, that edict remained firmly ingrained. So he had clamped his jaw shut and given the widow's white Persian cat its monthly dose of dewormer.

Luke was pumping gas by the time Danny Talbot stepped out the station door.

"Hey Luke, you know if you'd *fill* the tank for once, you wouldn't have to stop here so often."

"No time, Danny. Slim Brockett's got a ewe with a prolapse."

Danny made a sympathetic sound as he strolled toward the metal bucket filled with scummy water he kept beside the gas pump. Luke had often wondered what that mess would look like under a microscope. There was probably enough growth in it to start a new life form.

Without hesitation Danny plunged his hand into the bucket and pulled out a dripping rag. "P.J. wants to know if you can make it for supper tonight. Our kids are gonna forget what their godfather looks like."

Luke shook his head. "Tell her thanks, but if I'm not out on a call I'll be trying to catch an hour or two of sleep."

"You're gonna have to slow down." Danny wrung out the rag. "You're running yourself into the ground." He took a couple of halfhearted swipes across the dusty, bug-splattered windshield. Danny never exerted himself unnecessarily. "We could take staying up all night when we were in high school, but we're getting some years and mileage on us now." He pulled off his green seed corn cap and tilted his head down, showing off a bare circle of scalp surrounded by thinning, sandy-colored hair.

"Beautiful," Luke said with a grin. "You're getting bald and I'm getting gray." He ran a hand through his own hair, shaking out some of the road dust, recalling how shocked he'd been the morning he'd noticed the first gray hairs that now were liberally mixed with his original brown.

It still surprised him to be confronted with such blatant evidence of his advancing age. The inevitability of growing old didn't really bother him. It was just that he'd never envisioned doing it alone. And he'd always thought that one day he'd watch his own kids sing the National Anthem on the Ellison School stage where years ago his own awkward feet had once shuffled.

But things change.

And now looking back, it was hard to believe ten years had passed since Cassie McCabe dumped him.

One of the more fortunate days of his life, Luke thought, a wry smile tugging at the corners of his mouth. He shut off the pump and hung up the nozzle.

"Have any emergency calls last night?" Danny asked.

"Widow Simmons."

The two men looked at each other, both grimacing.

"I swear, if she calls me in the middle of the night again just because that cat of hers has a furball, I'm gonna say some words that'll make that woman choke on her fruitcake."

"Too bad she doesn't have that outhouse anymore," Danny said with dramatic remorsefulness.

They laughed together, and a special warmth that could only be generated by longtime friendship ran through Luke.

"Course, I'm the one who got in trouble for that prank," Danny complained. "Which you conned me into doing—as usual."

"How was I to know she was *in* the thing?" Luke screwed the gas cap back on. "She had indoor plumbing."

"Maybe she just used the outhouse when she was feeling sentimental." Danny stood with feet together, knees bent. He went through some free-throw motions, the limp rag smacking into the bucket of oil-slicked water. "Those parts for your truck came in." He'd been reminding Luke about the parts for the last three months.

Luke hopped in the truck and gave his friend the usual response. "I'll bring it in when things slow down. Put the gas on my tab." He pulled at the door, metal scraping against metal. Since it almost never latched the first time, Luke automatically groped for the outer handle, but Danny beat him to it.

"I'll fix the door, too." He slammed it shut, then braced his hands on the frame of the open window. "How's your grandmother doing? I love that nutty woman."

"I haven't had a chance to stop by her place this week, but I hope to hell she's keeping her nose out of trouble."

"You don't need to worry about her. Say, is she still wearing that coyote skin? That was sure wild when she came strolling into church with it on."

Luke's grandmother had caused quite a stir the first time she'd worn the pelt to the church's Christmas program, flinging it around her shoulders as if it was some priceless mink instead of a partially tanned hide that started to stink when combined too long with body heat.

"She must have put it away for the summer," Luke said. "I'm hoping she'll forget about it by fall."

"Hey," Danny said, as though just remembering something of extreme importance, "heard some news that might interest you." His eyes had taken on a distinctive glint. Luke knew what was coming. He'd seen that Jekyll and Hyde routine too many times. The inhabitants of Ellison, Iowa, whether young, old, male or female, thrived on gossip the way ticks thrive on blood.

"Got to go, Danny," he said quickly, hoping to escape before the tale began. He turned the ignition and pumped the gas pedal.

"Hear you have a new neighbor!" Danny shouted over the spastic roar of the poorly tuned engine.

Luke raised his eyebrows in question.

"Your tenant house. Heard somebody's movin' in there. A woman." Danny gave him a huge, exaggerated wink. "A *single* woman."

"What?" Luke couldn't believe he'd heard right. His grandmother was supposed to find a hired hand to live there.

"Yeah. Bud Campbell saw her when he was delivering mail. Figured you'd know all about it."

Luke let out a low moan. "No, I didn't." His grandmother was wearing him out. Only last week she'd brought some unsavory characters into her house and fed them. It wasn't that he was against charity, but they had shown their appreciation by helping themselves to whatever had caught their fancy. Luckily Luke had happened by just in time to find them loading the color television into their car while his grandmother stood by, wringing her hands. It was the only time Luke could recall seeing her look helpless, and he'd felt rage toward the people who'd taken advantage of her. He'd forced the thieves to put everything back and had been ready to turn them in to the county sheriff, but his grandmother had insisted that they hadn't been stealing, only borrowing a few items.

And here she was, at it again. Only this time she'd given the run of her tenant house to a total stranger. He sighed, thinking about the sleep he'd been looking forward to—the sleep he wasn't going to get now that he'd be spending his evening checking out this new freeloader, chasing her away if he had to.

He pushed in the clutch and shoved the gearshift into first.

"Tell your new neighbor hi for me," Danny said.

Luke growled deep in his throat, let out the clutch and pulled away, with Danny managing to slap the flat of his hand against the tailgate in a final farewell.

Luke was so wrapped up in worry about his grandmother's latest escapade that he missed the turnoff to Slim's. A curse escaped him as right front tire sank into a chuck hole, worn-out shocks causing the truck frame to jump and buck. He put in the clutch and tromped a booted foot down on the brake pedal, grinding to a stop. The truck whined as he reversed, jammed it into first, then made a quick left to rattle down the rutted lane.

He rummaged through the clutter on the dash, searching for his cigarettes. Then he remembered he'd quit smoking three months ago.

"Damn."

Jenny May stood in the second story bedroom, digging through her suitcase until she pulled out an oversize white cotton shirt. She slipped it on. The hem fell almost to the knees of her faded jeans, the loose clothing hiding her frailness and her bruises.

Hiding was something Jenny was good at. Over the years she had become a master at it, but until now she had only dealt with masking emotions—inner bruises, not outer ones.

The window was open and a breeze gently stirred the white ruffled curtains. She could hear birds squabbling in the lilac bush by the front walk. She could

smell the damp earth. The pinewood floor felt cool
under her bare feet.

A straight strand of dark, shoulder-length hair
slipped from the rubber band at the back of her head,
and she absentmindedly brushed it away from her too-
thin, too-pale face and heaved a contented sigh. Her
body ached and she was tired from her trip, but it was
a good kind of tired. Since the accident she'd been
jumpy and had been having trouble sleeping. She
hoped the solitude and peace of the country would
soothe her jangled nerves. And maybe she would be
able to get her appetite back and regain some of the
weight she'd lost.

Deciding to finish unpacking, she pulled out a
handful of folded clothes. A limp newspaper clipping
fluttered to the floor. She put the clothes on the bed
and picked up the scrap of paper. Even though she
knew the first paragraph by heart, she read it again.
The article was dated over two weeks earlier, June 20.

Aftershocks Of Earthquake Rock Mexico City.
Twenty-four-year-old Jennifer Elizabeth May, of
Miami Beach, Florida, was pulled from a col-
lapsed building after being trapped for three days.
The United Relief Group worker was found by a
search and rescue dog brought in from the United
States.

There was more to the article, but as always Jenny
stopped reading at that point and folded the paper

along the well-worn lines, her brown eyes growing large and distant. After five years with the United Relief disaster team she'd been temporarily laid off, told to take a leave of absence.

Traumatic neurosis.

In layman's terms the diagnosis translated to shellshock, which was totally ridiculous. Sure, she had trouble sleeping, and sudden noises made her jump, but in time that would pass.

But the head of her unit wouldn't listen to any of her arguments and had told her to go home, take it easy.

Home. For Jenny, there was really no such place. Her father was a successful stockbroker and her mother a Miami Beach socialite. Jenny had never fit into their glitzy lives and had actually been an embarrassment to her platinum-blond mother who must have thought that her daughter was a changeling... how else could she explain such a plain, sober child? When Jenny had announced at the age of nineteen that she was leaving the finishing school chosen by her mother to become a lowly aid in a United Relief unit, both her parents had turned their backs on her.

But when her mother, Sancha May, had read about the earthquake in the *Miami Herald*, she'd phoned the hospital to inquire about her daughter. Jenny had quickly assured her that she was okay, knowing that her mother's relief at the news was largely due to finding that she wouldn't be saddled with an injured daughter.

End of conversation.

So Jenny had left Mexico with no plans for her im-
mediate future, no idea of where she would stay until
she could return to work. Upon arriving in the States
she checked the post office box she kept in Tampa and
found a letter from Stella Tate, a somewhat eccentric
and utterly charming old woman Jenny had struck up
an acquaintance with a few years before when they
shared adjacent airplane seats. It seemed Stella had
read about the earthquake and Jenny's accident and
was inviting Jenny to stay on her Iowa farm for the
summer. She had an empty house in desperate need of
an occupant "to keep the rodents away." Her quaint
offer had seemed a godsend to Jenny.

Stella had even gone so far as to pick her up at the
bus station in an old black car with running boards,
round fenders and scratchy wool upholstery that
smelled of mothballs. An hour ago, when the small,
bustling woman had dropped her off at the two-story
farmhouse, she'd chirped that she would leave Jenny
to rest up and they could have a chat tomorrow when
she was settled.

Jenny loved the house. It was comfortable, with lots
of woodwork and walls papered with tiny flowered
prints, paste waxed floors and hand-braided throw
rugs. She hadn't expected anything like this. Even the
bed was made, complete with fresh-smelling quilts and
plump feather pillows. And not a sign of a single ro-
dent.

The sound of a vehicle on the gravel road drew Jenny out of her reflections. She was a little surprised to hear it slow and then stop in front of the house, accompanied by what sounded like metal scraping against metal. She was waiting for a knock when the front door opened and closed.

Stella must have decided to come back.

But then, incredibly, from directly below her, heavy footfalls sounded against the wooden floor. Jenny stood perfectly still, listening. The footsteps passed the bottom of the stairs and continued fading toward the back of the house, into the proximity of the kitchen. Paper rustled, then she heard the sound of a refrigerator being opened and closed.

Whoever it was certainly wasn't trying to be quiet. Obviously it wasn't a thief. Maybe Stella had called a repairman about something. That made sense. Maybe the refrigerator needed attention.

Before she could change her mind, she gathered her courage and hurried downstairs, her small bare feet skimming the bowed wooden steps.

Turning the corner, she practically barreled into the broad chest of the man coming through the kitchen doorway. He was carrying a can of beer and a bag of potato chips.

"There's more beer in the refrigerator," he said almost absentmindedly, popping the tab on the beer. His gaze went from the can in his hand to her face. For a fraction of a second it seemed as if a spark of something flashed in his eyes, then he was edging past her.

Jenny watched in stunned amazement as he continued into the living room. He switched on the TV, then plopped his large muscular frame down in the overstuffed chair, nudging the footstool closer with the toe of one boot.

The sound and picture came on. "*Green Acres*," he commented, stretching his long, jean-clad legs to the stool, crossing his feet at the ankles. "I love Arnold." He tilted his head back and took a long drink of beer, then opened the bag of chips. "One smart pig."

All Jenny could do was stand in the doorway and try to keep her mouth from going slack. This was *Twilight Zone* material. She remembered seeing an episode where a person could simply walk through walls and become a part of total strangers' lives.

"What's for supper?" The words were casually tossed over the man's broad shoulder, as if he took her presence for granted, as if this were routine for them both.

She stared at the back of his head. Wavy, dusty hair fell almost to the neckband of a blue T-shirt. His hair color would probably be called medium brown, except for the long sun-bleached strands running through it.

Jenny finally found her voice. "What are you doing here?"

"Great!" He pointed his beer toward the TV. "This is the episode where Arnold gets amnesia."

Enough was enough.

Jenny strode into the room, flicked off the television and turned to glare at him, arms crossed at her waist, one hip out, a small bare foot tapping the floor in front of her. "Who are you, and what are you doing here?" she demanded. Her voice came out loud and angry, but slightly shaky.

The man looked up, eyes bland. "You mean my grandmother didn't explain it to you?"

"What are you talking about?"

"I'm Lucas Tate. Stella's grandson."

The bad feeling she'd had ever since she'd heard his footsteps in the house intensified tenfold. "And?"

"I guess you could say I come with the house." He paused. "I live here."

She let out a strangled gasp.

He popped another potato chip into his mouth, regarding her as he chewed, assessing her reaction.

"Wh-what are you talking about?" she stammered.

"Are you sure she didn't tell you?"

All Jenny could manage was a slow shake of her head.

"Hey, she didn't use that line about having an empty house and needing somebody to live in it to keep the rats away, did she?" He laughed and the sound echoed off the papered walls. "Just between you and me—" he winked "—Stella's a tad peculiar. Some grandmothers like to bake apple pies for their grandsons. Stella likes to bring me women." He took another drink of beer.

That was the most absurd thing Jenny had ever heard. "I don't believe you," she bluffed. "Stella wouldn't do that." Then she had an uncomfortable recollection: the time on the airplane...Stella had been wearing the oddest stole...some strange kind of animal fur Jenny had never seen before.

He shrugged as if to say it made no difference whether she believed him or not. "Turn the set back on and move to the left, will you? I've never seen the end of this show, and I want to find out if Arnold gets his memory back."

She stayed where she was.

"I like that big shirt. Bet it would look really nice if you turned on the TV and stayed right there. Backlighting, you know."

His eyes had lost their indifference. Now they were roaming over every line of her slim body.

She dropped her hands to her sides, fingers curling into tight fists. "I'll just call your grandmother and find out about this!" She marched to the kitchen where she'd seen a wall phone. No phone book. She opened and shut drawers until she found a phone book no thicker than a slice of diet bread. Quickly she ruffled through the pages. Tate...Tate... She ran her index finger down the columns. Lucas Tate. She jabbed at the name. She checked the number in the book, then looked up at the black wall phone. The numbers were different. Which meant Lucas Tate *didn't* live here.

Her eyes went back to the book in her hand. Stella's number was the only other Tate. She anchored the receiver under her chin and had dialed two numbers when a brown hand reached around the corner, one finger pushing down the phone's metal cradle.

"Don't bother Stella."

Lucas Tate's voice and demeanor had done a complete turnaround. No longer did he appear bored. His voice was deep and ominous, his expression hostile. He slipped the receiver from her lax grasp and hung it up.

At first she'd been confused, even irritated by him, but now that he was towering over her, now that he was close enough for her to see the anger coiled in the depths of eyes the color of a tropical ocean, she was afraid. And so she called upon her talent for putting up false fronts, false shows of bravery. "Get out of here!"

"Not until you tell me what you're doing in my grandmother's house."

"Stella invited me."

"I know, but what's in it for you? Let's face it. This is no vacation hot spot. Why would a single woman want to come to a rural place like this? It doesn't add up."

"It's a private matter." Again she clenched her fists, her fingernails digging into her palms. She didn't want to talk about her problems. Didn't want to talk about what had happened to her, or why she had no other place to go. "I don't have to explain anything to you."

"I look out for Stella, because Stella doesn't always look out for herself. She trusts everybody, and people take advantage of that trust."

"A little trust might not be a bad quality for you to work on."

He smiled, but the smile didn't reach his eyes. Then he took a step forward.

Jenny took a step back.

"The last person who used this place invited two hundred people here for a four day party," he said grimly. "By the time I got back to town and kicked them out, five thousand dollars' worth of damage had been done."

"I assure you, I'm not that kind of person."

"That's what Stella's last charity case said."

"I'm not a charity case. Stella *invited* me here," she repeated.

He took another step forward, and this time kept coming until Jenny's spine was pressed against the metal trim that edged the counter. He stood so close that she could feel the heat generated by his tense body, smell the outdoor scent trapped in his shirt. Fresh panic washed over her. She felt as defenseless as a child. He was so big; she was so small.

He was so different from the men she was used to—suit and tie types, or bright, idealistic boys learning to be adults. Lucas Tate was so rugged, earthy, angry....

Her heart hammered against her rib cage. Perspiration broke out on her skin. She gripped the edge of the counter behind her and nervously moistened her dry lips, unable to tear her gaze from his.

The anger in his eyes subtly changed. His pupils grew larger. A small jolt went through her as his hand brushed her arm, the hard calluses on his fingertips barely skimming her overheated skin. She felt as if she couldn't breathe, as if somebody was squeezing the air from her lungs.

His eyes were very blue, turquoise blue. The tops of his eyebrows were bleached from the sun, his day's growth of beard peppered with blond hairs among the brown. She was surprised to see gray in his hair—he seemed too young.

Next thing she knew, his hands were on her waist, his head bending toward her. Then she felt his warm breath caress her lips just before his mouth pressed over hers. . . .

Jenny's knees went weak, and she had the oddest sensation in her stomach—a fluttering. She clung to the counter to keep from giving in to the sudden over-whelming urge to raise her hands to his shoulders. A series of small tremors coursed through her.

As abruptly as he'd begun the kiss, he stopped, re-leased her and took a step back, watching her, his expression thoughtful, almost a little puzzled. But maybe he wasn't puzzled. Maybe he always frowned like that.

She could only stare back, feeling dazed, confused. A hot blush stole into her cheeks when she realized what she'd just done: for a second, she'd kissed him back. Jenny didn't go around kissing strange men. Or letting strange men kiss her. In fact, she'd only been kissed, *really* kissed, a couple of times in her life, and it had been nothing like this. Nothing at all. And now here she was, kissing a man she'd never set eyes on until five minutes ago.

"Get out of here!" As soon as she'd spoken, she clamped her lips together to stop their trembling.

He stood there, watching her, taking careful note of her flushed cheeks, her flushed mouth. "Okay."

His answer surprised her. She hadn't expected him to give in so easily.

He walked to the kitchen door and stopped, hand poised on the latch, curiosity still in his eyes. "You can keep the beer and chips." Then he gave her a dazzling, ornery smile that made her heart turn over in her chest.

But on the outside, she remained calm. She crossed her arms at her waist and lifted her chin a little higher, feigning disinterest as she waited for him to leave, all the while terribly aware of the tingly impression his lips had left on hers, all the while aware of each fast, thudding beat of her heart.

"See you around?"

"I hope not."

He smiled again, as if to say: *we'll see.* Then he stepped outside, the screen door banging behind him.

Jenny lunged across the kitchen, slammed the heavy inner door and shot the bolt, thankful that there were

only two Tates in the phone book. She didn't want to
have to worry about running into any more of Stella's
relatives.

Chapter Two

The phone was ringing, but Luke didn't want to be disturbed. He was dreaming about a girl with dark hair and dark eyes. She had made a dandelion chain and was laughing up at him as she tried to put it around his neck. Luke was enjoying the dream. It gave him a good feeling.

But the darn phone kept ringing. In his sleep, he dreamed he answered it. Lying flat on his back, he dreamed that he stretched his arm up to the dresser until his groping fingers touched the receiver and lifted it to his ear.

The ringing persisted.

Luke opened his eyes just enough to make out that it was daytime, but he hadn't the remotest idea whether it was morning, noon or early evening. All he knew was that he felt as though he'd been run over by a truck, and the blasted phone was still ringing. Outside, the dogs were barking.

He looked up at the dresser. No phone. He looked down at the littered floor. The telephone cord trailed across the hardwood, disappearing under the clothes he'd worn last night.

Luke groaned and let his head drop to the bed.

At three in the morning Jake Chapman had called him to help deliver a colt. The delivery had gone smoothly, but motherhood had definitely brought out the protective instinct in the mare and since Luke's relfexes were never good at that hour he'd come away from Chapman's with at least two cracked ribs. But then, injuries went along with being a vet. And the bigger the animal, the bigger the injury. He supposed he was lucky it had been his ribs instead of his head. He'd been out of commission for a week the time a horse had kicked him in the head.

He put a hand to the heated flesh of his bruised side. Wincing, he reached down and pulled at the cord, tugging the still-ringing phone toward him across the floor, his mud-stained shirt coming with it.

"Yeah..." he muttered into the mouthpiece.

"Luke?"

His grandmother's voice blared out of the receiver with such volume that he had to hold it away from his ear.

"Did I wake you, Lucas?"

He ran a hand through his hair and eased himself back against the headboard of the bed. "No, Grandma."

"You're late," she said accusingly. "And don't call me Grandma. People will start thinking I'm senile—or that you're going through a second childhood."

He smiled indulgently. "Okay, *Stella*."

He was late. Late for what? He tried to get his groggy mind in gear. He couldn't even remember what day of the week it was.

"You didn't forget about Sunday dinner, did you?"

Sunday. He turned his head to look at the luminous digits on the bedside clock. 12:02. No wonder the dogs were barking. They were hungry.

"I didn't forget," he assured her. "I had a couple of calls last night and overslept. I'll be right out."

"Well, hurry," Stella told him. "I baked all your favorite things."

"Stella, I love you."

After hanging up the phone, he lay on his back for a few minutes, waiting for the blood to start moving through his veins a little faster. While he waited, he found himself thinking about the girl he'd met yesterday.

One thing for sure, he'd made a big mistake—a major error in judgement. As soon as he'd kissed her, he'd realized she wasn't the kind of girl you just grab and kiss, which meant she wasn't the kind to have wild parties either.

It wasn't that she couldn't kiss. She could. When he'd felt her soft lips begin to move under his, his heart had raced and his body temperature had risen several notches. No, it was her reaction that gave her away. She'd been flustered, embarrassed.

A frown creased his brow. When he'd held her, he'd felt a frailty her clothes had hidden, and when he'd looked into her doe-like eyes, he'd seen that the darkness beneath them wasn't caused by smudged mascara.

Who was she? And what was she doing in Ellison, Iowa, where all the residents knew one another's religious preferences, bank account numbers and birthdays? It just didn't add up.

Still thinking about her, Luke dragged himself out of bed, limped downstairs, fed the animals and showered, then headed for his grandmother's.

The ride in his pickup was no picnic. He hadn't been able to get the bandage tight enough to keep his ribs from shifting with every bounce. But once he reached his grandmother's two-story farmhouse he was careful to walk normally in case she was watching from a window. His constant injuries upset her.

He opened the door to the enclosed porch, almost stepping on Stella's huge gray house rabbit, Mr. Bun. "What did you do to get banished to the porch?" Luke asked, careful of his side as he squatted down to pet the soft animal. "Been chewing lamp cords again? Or terrorizing the cats?"

Luke straightened and put his hand to the kitchen doorknob. He looked down. Mr. Bun was poised, nose to the crack in the door, ready to dash in as soon as it opened. "Oh, no you don't, you furry hoodlum." Luke gently pushed him back with a booted foot. "Go play in your litter box or I'll sic Mr. McGregor on you."

He opened the door just far enough to slip inside. Fantastic smells greeted him, evidence of his grandmother's home cooking. The round oak table was set with a white, pressed tablecloth and embroidered napkins. The window above the sink was open, and fresh air drifted in, mixing with the smells of food.

Sunday dinner at his grandmother's was a tradition, but there had been a time when Luke had spent Sundays quite differently. When he was ten and living with his divorced mother in Detroit, she'd labeled him a juvenile delinquent and declared him totally unmanageable. Then she'd given him the choice of being sent to reform school or to his Grandma Stella's in Iowa. It wasn't because his mother and widowed grandmother were good friends. No, Luke had always suspected he'd been sent to Stella's out of spite, but something had backfired.

At a time when it seemed as if Luke's world was crashing in around him, Stella had welcomed him with open arms, making him feel special, wanted. Under her care, he grew big and strong, but most of all he learned to vent his energies in more constructive directions. If it hadn't been for Stella, he'd most likely be doing time right now.

Luke went directly to the oven, opened the door and peered in.

Roast beef.

Soft footsteps sounded from the adjoining living room.

He decided to come right out and tell Stella about yesterday, give her his side of the story before she heard someone else's. "I met your new tenant," Luke called over his shoulder, shutting the oven door. "Just stopped by to get acquainted. You might as well know right off, since you'll find out soon enough—I kissed her." He lifted the lid from the pan on the stove.

Turnips. He loved turnips. "And yes, I liked it."

The floor creaked and he looked up.

It was a good thing he didn't embarrass easily. *She* was standing in the doorway, the person with the big brown eyes, the person he'd kissed yesterday. The person whose name he didn't even know.

Today she was wearing an old-fashioned dress with tiny flowers on it. High neck . . . knees covered.

He put the lid back on the turnips, then leaned against the counter edge, crossed his arms over his chest and racked his brain for something witty to say. He couldn't think of a darn thing, so he just smiled at her.

She didn't smile back. "Stella invited me to dinner, but she didn't mention anything about her ill-mannered grandson being here. If I'd known, I would have declined."

"Speaking of my grandmother, where is she?"

"Upstairs. Changing out of her church clothes." The words came grudgingly, as if she would have preferred not to talk to him at all.

The floor above their heads creaked. Luke unfurled his arms and took a couple of steps toward her, stopping when she stiffened. "We've got to do this fast before she gets back."

He tugged his shirttail from his jeans, then began unbuttoning the shirt, watching her eyes growing wider with each unfastened button.

"Wh-what are you doing?"

"Doing? Why, taking off my shirt." Moving stiffly, he eased his arms out and tossed the cotton shirt over the back of the spindle chair. Around his torso, like some unsightly cummerbund, was the twelve inch wide elastic bandage he'd attempted to wind around himself after his shower. "I couldn't get this thing tight enough by myself." Deftly, he removed the four metal clips.

He heard her expelled breath. "You expect *me* to do it?" she asked, disbelief in her voice and face. "I think you'd better wait until Stella comes back downstairs."

"I don't want Stella to know about it. Now come on. Hurry up. You don't want her to get upset, do you?"

He could see the inner struggle she was waging and was amused by it.

"Okay," she finally said, "but I'm just doing this for Stella."

Her words may have been spoken defiantly, but when she approached him it was with caution, like some wary, half-wild animal.

He held his arms away from his body, elbows bent, one hand on the bandage to keep it from slipping off completely. He could tell she wasn't at all eager to be this close to him, let alone touch him, *help* him.

"I can't believe I'm doing this." Her cold finger-tips accidently came in contact with his warm, soap-scented flesh.

"Youch! Your hands are like ice," he complained.

"Then I'll try very hard to not touch you."

"Touch me all you want. I don't mind."

"But I'll mind."

"So you *say*."

Hands on hips, she glared up at him. "Do you want me to help you or not?"

"Okay, I'll be good." He smiled broadly. "And when I'm good, I'm very, very good."

She clicked her tongue, then bent her head to look at the bandage. "This will have to be taken off and started over."

"Whatever you think," he said docilely.

He looked down at the top of her head. Her hair was shiny, and he could see white skin where it parted, making him think of a child. He inhaled. She smelled fresh and clean, like Ivory soap. He could feel her soft breath caressing his bare arm, hear her sharp gasp when the bandage fell away to reveal his injury in all its black and blue glory.

"How on earth did you get this?"

He strained to see. It was even darker than it had been earlier. Unsightly was the word that sprang to mind. He shrugged. "Let's just say I spent a wild night with a wild filly who liked things rough." Luke could never stay docile very long.

She glanced up, then away, but not before he saw the color that rose in her pale cheeks. He started to laugh, but the sound was quickly silenced as pain darted up his side, cutting off his wind. He let out his breath, forcing himself to breathe shallowly.

"Serves you right," she said unsympathetically. "No wonder you didn't want Stella to know." She concentrated on wrapping the bandage, indicating that he should turn around, her fingers skimming his skin as they smoothed the cloth. In his mind, he pictured her hands on him.... Then he just naturally thought about how her lips had opened under his yesterday, all soft and warm....

Clipped footsteps sounded above them, reminding him of the business at hand. "Come on, as tight as you can, now."

"Gladly."

She pulled and before he could stop it, a grunt of pain escaped his lips.

"I'm sorry!" she whispered, sounding horrified at what she'd done.

He smiled. "That's okay. It has to be tight." He handed her a metal clip. Her small hands trembled slightly when they brushed against his hard palm.

When she was done, he snatched up his shirt and had just finished tucking in the tails when Stella bustled in. She was wearing a gauzy outfit that looked like something he might have seen in the window of Cook's Antiques. Her silver hair was pulled up on top of her head in what she had once told him was called a Gibson Girl Style.

"I see you've met Jenny."

Jenny.

So, that was her name. He liked it. It suited her.

"Jenny May," his grandmother said. "May being her last name, not middle."

"*May?* What the hell kind of name is that?" he asked, secretly deciding he liked it too.

"Lucas Tate! Mind your manners. You're not too big for me to throttle."

Barely standing five feet tall in her sturdy black shoes, his grandmother glared up at him, blue eyes flashing behind silver-rimmed glasses, hands on her slight hips. The expression she was wearing was one he didn't believe he'd seen since he was a kid. Not since the time he'd cut up her embroidered sheets so he could doctor Danny's dog. She probably would have taken the whole thing better if Rufus had really been injured. Luke had tried to explain to her that in order to become a vet, a person had to know such things beforehand, but he'd been sent to his room anyway.

"You be nice to Jenny. She's not tough-skinned like your Cassie was."

"She was never *my* Cassie," Luke said with irritation.

Stella looked at Jenny, then said in a confiding voice, "Cassie was his high school sweetheart. At one time, they were all set to get married."

"Stella—" Luke warned.

"But when she found out he planned on living here in the sticks instead of the big city, she dumped him like yesterday's oatmeal."

Luke growled and turned his back on them both. He grabbed a pair of hotpads off the counter, opened the oven door and took out the roast.

"Don't mind him," Stella went on in a husky whisper that was louder than her natural voice. "Even though he can be an ornery rapscallion, he's got the softest heart of any man I ever knew."

Luke gave his grandmother the kind of look that sent most people running. She smiled affectionately at him in return. He focused his attention on slicing the roast.

Luke knew that Stella thought he harbored a grudge against women. But it wasn't true. He didn't feel any bitterness toward Cassie. He just didn't want to get serious about anybody, because he didn't want to have to make a choice between getting married and staying in Ellison.

Bloom where you're planted, that was his belief. This was his home, these were his people and even if he wasn't an actual native, he considered himself one. Maybe that's why Ellison was so special to him. Maybe he could see its magic because he hadn't always lived here.

"When Lucas was little, he was always bringing home some injured wild animal or other," Stella said. "I remember a baby deer he found once. Its mother must have died, and the poor thing was almost dead. But he fed it from a eyedropper and then a bottle till it got well enough to run loose in the yard. It used to sleep curled up on the front porch, even when it got full-grown."

Her voice dropped, but he could still hear every word. "Then one day it was gone. Luke was heartbroken—worrying that hunters might have gotten it, you know."

Luke turned, planning to ask his grandmother to keep the rest of her stories to herself, when his gaze was arrested.

Jenny's huge, liquid eyes were focused on his face, her fingers gripping the back rail of the spindle chair. He totally lost track of what he was going to say. The words just deserted his mind as he was struck by the intensity of her expression, by the sadness, the *pity*.

Pity. That was it. Exactly what Stella was trying to do, he realized with fresh exasperation. Get Jenny to feel sorry for him. It wasn't going to work. He could be just as stubborn as Stella.

"Okay. What do you say we put away the violins and hankies and eat?"

"Doesn't he get riled over the silliest things?" Stella asked.

They had made it about halfway through the meal when Luke was driven to ask, "Just out of curiosity, where on earth did you get that outfit? It looks like something from the Roaring Twenties."

"Why thank you, Luke," Stella said with a smile. "I got it at a secondhand store."

He put down his fork and leaned toward her. "You don't need to get clothes from a secondhand store."

"I know that. I don't happen to like any of the new styles, and synthetic fabrics give me hives."

"I like your dress," Jenny said.

"Thank you, dear."

"And I liked the one you wore to church."

"I did wonder if the boa wasn't a little much for summertime...."

"Well...that could be."

"Boone Bailey gave it to me. He collects ginseng and all sorts of wonderful natural things from the woods. And cans. He collects cans and gets the most marvelous exercise walking along the highway. That's where Boone found my boa."

Luke began choking and startled laughter burst from Jenny before she could stop it. She clapped a hand to her mouth and fell weakly against the back of her chair. Luke reached for his glass, fierce watery eyes glaring at Stella over the rim.

"My God!" he finally roared when he'd quit choking. "You mean to tell me that thing you've been wearing around your neck is a *road kill*?"

"Don't raise your voice to me," Stella said indignantly. "How can Boone get one any other way? You steal the poor man's traps as soon as he puts them down! And you yell at him. Boone isn't used to people who yell. He doesn't realize that you don't really mean it."

"I *do* mean it. He's a sneak. He sets his traps on my property."

"Trapping is an important part of his livelihood."

"I won't have anybody trapping my land! There's been too much trapping done in the past few years."

"Excuse me." Stella patted the corners of her mouth, then put her napkin down next to her plate. "It's getting too loud in here. I'll have to go take out my hearing aid if you're going to be this loud."

"Hearing aid? Since when do you wear a hearing aid!"

Stella frowned at him, then got up and glided from the room saying, "A soft answer turneth away wrath."

"Oh, good Lord." He looked at Jenny. "She's always quoting proverbs at me. Provoke not your children!" he shouted at the empty doorway.

With Stella gone, the kitchen became uncomfortably quiet. Jenny picked up her fork, but what little appetite she'd had was gone.

Luke took a bite of potatoes, then noticed Jenny wasn't eating. "Go ahead and eat. Don't worry about

Stella. She'll be back in a minute. She likes to play games.''

"I, ah...I just can't eat any more." Jenny put down her fork and pushed her plate back. The days she'd spent without food had caused her stomach to shrink, and it was still difficult for her to eat much at one time.

His eyebrows drew together but she was thankful that he didn't press her.

"So, tell me," Luke said, pushing his own plate away. "Where you from?"

"Is this another interrogation?" She forced herself to look directly at him, meeting the challenge in his eyes. She wouldn't let him intimidate her.

He scooted his chair closer, leaning an elbow on the table, a matter of inches separating them. He was too close. She was getting that funny tingly feeling again, like she'd had yesterday when he'd touched her, when he'd— Quickly she leaned away, the rungs of the chair back pressing into her spine. "I'm from Florida—Miami Beach."

His eyes narrowed. "A city slicker?"

"If you say so." She shrugged, hoping to convey a bit of nonchalance. "Actually, I haven't lived there in several years."

"Where have you lived?"

She decided to give him enough information to satisfy his curiosity. Then maybe he would leave her alone. "I work for United Relief—it's similar to the Red Cross, so I travel quite a bit."

"Then what are you doing here?"

She looked down at her clenched hands. "Taking a vacation."

"In Ellison, Iowa?" he asked in disbelief. "Hicksville, U.S.A.?"

"I like it here. It's quiet."

"It's boring."

"That depends on your definition of boring."

"They roll up the roads at six o'clock."

"I won't be going anywhere."

"We don't get cable, and the closest theater is the Roxy in Spring Grove—great example of art deco. If you go there, be sure to wear old clothes and old shoes. And better bring something to read in case the film breaks—which it always does." He paused, thinking. "'Course, there are a few things that might be worth taking in while you're here."

"Oh?"

A teasing glint shone from the depths of his turquoise eyes. "The mule-jumping contest and the bathtub races." He nodded. "Darned exciting. Not as exciting as watching Delbert Kline rotate the tires on his Winnebago, mind you, but exciting."

Laughter burst from Jenny. She was still laughing when Stella returned.

"I'm so glad to see you getting along so well," she said approvingly. "I must admit I had my doubts. Luke can be a trifle..."

Luke threw his grandmother a pained look.

"A trifle *feisty*."

Feisty? Feisty was a word used to describe an unruly child, not a grown man.

Just then the phone rang. "Luke, it's for you." Stella handed the receiver to him. "It's Kelly," she added with a loud whisper.

Luke leaned against the counter, his voice suddenly pure honey, full of warmth and smiles. "No, I didn't forget." A pause. A chuckle. "Now, sweetheart, when have I ever forgotten you?"

Sweetheart?

Jenny tried not to listen, but it was impossible with him standing only a few feet from her. She stared down at the tablecloth, suddenly feeling tired and a little sick. She dimly wondered if she was coming down with something.

Who was Kelly? The person he'd been with last night, the one he'd gotten in a fight over?

"I'll be there in ten minutes." Luke hung up. "I've got to go."

"What about the apple pie?"

"I'll stop by later." Putting an arm around his grandmother, he bent down and kissed her lined cheek.

The simple show of affection touched a chord of longing in Jenny. She could sense the strong bond between them. Luke, fiercely protective; Stella, full of a grandmother's unconditional love for her big, untempered grandson. In Jenny's household there had never been any displays of affection. There hadn't been any displays of anything. According to her mother, emotional displays were a sign of poor breeding.

"Sorry I couldn't stay to help with the dishes this time." Luke tossed Jenny a floursack towel and she caught it to her. "But I'll just bet anything our Jenny here can handle a dishtowel."

Our Jenny.

Had he been consciously aware of what he'd said? Nobody had ever said those words before. She liked the way it sounded. She was still thinking about it after he left.

The older woman gathered up the dirty dishes while Jenny collected the glasses. "I wish that grandson of mine would slow down and quit working so hard," Stella said, worry in her voice. "I keep telling him it's going without sleep that gets him hurt. His reflexes get slow and he can't think as fast." She put the dishes in the sudsy dishwater. "Last year at this time he was kicked in the head by a half-wild horse and didn't recognize anybody for a week."

Kicked by a horse... A *filly*?

Everything fell into place for Jenny. The animal stories...the filly...Luke's bruised side. Even though she was sure she knew the answer, she asked, "What does Luke do for a living?"

"Why, dear, I thought he told you. He's a veterinarian," Stella said with pride. "He won't even slow down on Sundays. Right now he's gone to help Kelly get her goat ready for the 4-H county fair."

A strange sense of relief washed over Jenny. 4-H. Children were in 4-H. *Kelly was a little girl.*

She picked up a plate and began drying it, thinking about how nice it was to be here, to be around somebody like Stella. A warm, open-arms kind of person. The kind of person who called people dear and honey and sweetheart. Cozy words.

And not quite as consciously she thought about a most infuriating man, a man who had called her "our Jenny."

Stella looked up from the sink. "It's so nice to see you smiling. Now, didn't I say coming here would do you good?"

Chapter Three

Terror enshrouded Jenny, wrapping its constricting tentacles around her heart. She'd fallen into a black abyss that had closed after her, blocking all light, entombing her. She forced herself to draw a shallow breath, the dead, dirt-laden air scorching her lungs.

It was a dream; Jenny knew it was a dream, yet that knowledge didn't make it any less horrible, didn't make it seem any less real. She told herself that all she had to do was wake up and the dream would stop.

Then the same thing happened that always happened: she opened her eyes to complete darkness, her short-lived relief giving way to shock at recognizing that she was still caught within the clutches of her nightmare.

It wasn't the darkness alone that made the blood pulse through her head like thundering hooves, made her breath come short and rasping. Like a magician's cloak, the darkness concealed what lurked beneath it. And that unseen, pervasive presence was close, very close, of that she was certain. So close she dared not move for fear she might brush up against it.

Run. Get away.

She tried to move, but her body was trapped by the weight of the darkness, by the ominous sleeping presence.

It's a dream. A *dream*.

She struggled with her terror. If she allowed it to take over, she might never wake up, never get out.

On her fourth morning in Ellison, as on all the previous mornings, Jenny came awake sitting bolt upright, heart racing, body coated with cold sweat. With an open palm, she pressed the sheets to her chest, fighting for air, fighting the unknown fear that consumed her.

Upon awakening, she could never recall what the nightmare had been about, could never visualize a single part of it. All that was left was the feeling—and the feeling was one of heart-stopping terror.

As always, she waited for the residue of the dream to fall from her mind until it was just a lingering cobweb. And as always, she sternly told herself to forget about it, that in time the dreams would stop. It was only to be expected that someone who had been trapped underground for three days would have nightmares. She just hoped they would end soon. It seemed that nowadays she woke up more exhausted than when she'd gone to bed. In the evenings she would find herself fighting sleep, but it was a losing battle, because eventually sleep always won.

Beside her, the bedside lamp she'd left on all night glowed feebly. She reached over and flicked it off, her sore, bruised body protesting. Outside, in the morning light, birds chattered, and the sound was comforting.

All three bedroom windows were open, the box fan was humming in the corner, and yet the air in the room felt heavy and damp, portending another hot, sultry day.

Jenny shut off the fan, then went into the bathroom and took a shower, knowing from experience that the hot water would soothe away the soreness in her body. Then, even though it was too hot for them, she slipped on a light, loose pair of jeans to hide the dark bruise on her thigh. She had the same problem with a top. She ended up wearing a white poplin shirt. After cuffing the short sleeves, she checked in the mirror to make sure the discoloration on her collarbone was covered. Then, hardly giving more than a fleeting thought to breakfast, she slipped on a pair of jogging shoes, ran a brush through her straight, shoulder-length hair and went downstairs and out the back door.

She loved the yard. There was a huge maple tree with a branch that was just right for a swing. Climb-

ing roses and clematis vines trailed up white lattice-
work to the slanting green porch roof. Someone had
planted petunias in the space between the house and
the uneven sidewalk, and at night their sweet fragrance drifted in the open windows on dew-laden air.
The clover-and-dandelion-littered grass was like a
thick carpet. Whenever she went barefoot, it felt cool
against the soles of her feet. Stella had called the dandelions pesky weeds, but Jenny liked them for their
bright cheerfulness. Her mother's lawn had been
strictly for show, certainly not a place to be enjoyed,
not a place for a child to play. It had taken the skill of
a full-time gardener to keep the growth within Sancha May's rigidly set boundaries.

Deciding to look in the barn, Jenny moved down the
slope and across the gravel drive. At first the massive
hanging barn door didn't want to move. She tugged at
the metal handle, her knees bending with the effort.
Finally wheels squeaked and the door rolled open
enough for her to look inside.

It was cool and dark and quiet—like a tomb.

And suddenly the same dark, nameless fear she'd
felt upon waking washed over her again. She leaned
into the door, pushing with all her weight. This time
the door glided all the way open, bathing the barn in
light, the oppressive sensation lifting from her at the
same time.

She let out a small, relieved sigh, straightened, then
stepped inside, the soles of her tennis shoes whisper-
ing through the loose straw.

It wasn't a very big barn. One side was stacked to the rafters with small rectangular bales of hay. Jenny decided right then and there that hay smelled wonderful. Until now her favorite smell had always been that of the ocean. But this was every bit as nice in a different way. Where the scent of the ocean was bold and free, this was earthy and comforting.

She walked to the ladder and grasped its side rails, thinking to climb high enough to look in the loft, when she spotted a dust-covered boy's bicycle sticking out from behind some of the hay.

A bike. It had been years since she'd been on a bike.

Jenny let go of the ladder and went over to the bicycle, wiping her hand across the seat to uncover a red letter *S*. Her hand came away smudged and trailing with cobwebs.

A memory came out of nowhere, something she had completely forgotten until now: she pictured her eight-year-old fingers with their chewed fingernails carefully clothespinning gold-edged playing cards to the spokes of her bicycle. When she'd finished attaching the entire deck, she'd settled herself on the banana seat and roared off down the street, pigtails flying straight behind her, plastic streamers on the handlebars snapping in the wind. For a few minutes it had been wonderful—magical, just as she'd imagined flying to be, only better.

But Jenny could always count on her mother to bring her back down to earth. When she'd stopped in front of the house to catch a breath, Sancha May had been waiting to commandeer the bike. She had jabbed a long, lacquered nail at Jenny's nose, and in an icy, controlled voice she'd called her an uncouth tomboy.

It turned out that the cards weren't the kind you thoughtlessly toss in a shopping cart on Dollar Day. These had been special, trimmed in fourteen-karat gold. That was the last time Jenny had been on a bicycle.

Now she eyed the rusty bike with something like longing. It wasn't the bulky, heavy kind like Miss Gulch, the Wicked Witch of the West, rode, but it wasn't a light touring model either. With its handbrakes and three speeds, it fell somewhere in between.

The idea came to her that she could ride to the grocery store in Ellison. Stella had taken her shopping in Spring Grove, but that had been before Jenny had seen the scrawny gray striped kitten slinking around the barn. She had set out a bowl of bread and milk, but she needed to get some cat food.

And besides, she'd like to go into Ellison. The only glimpse she'd had of the small town had been four days ago when Stella had picked her up at the bus station. On the way back, they had putted down the block of false-fronted buildings, Stella boasting that there wasn't a single traffic light in the whole of Jefferson County.

Looking in the barber shop window, Jenny had seen a little blond-haired boy getting his hair cut. Outside, two old men stood talking and laughing. And she had thought how nice it must be to live in a place where life didn't rush at you before you saw it coming. It was comforting to know there were places like Ellison, places where children could go for walks by themselves, where older people could stand on corners and talk without being thoughtlessly jostled.

Jenny pressed her thumb against the bike's front tire, testing it. The dry, stiff rubber sank all the way to the rusty rim. A red hand pump hung from a nail on the wall, so she took it down, hoping the tires had merely deflated over the years.

Fifteen minutes later the tires were holding air, the bike had been wiped somewhat clean, and Jenny had even strapped a wicker basket to the handlebars. She walked the bike out of the barn, swung a leg over the frame and took off down the driveway and past the mailbox, feeling quite pleased with herself.

The road to Ellison was actually more dust than gravel, which made pedaling easier. And while the exhilaration wasn't up to what Jenny had felt as a child, it still brought the start of a smile to her lips and made her feel more in tune with the world than she had in some time.

She slowed down so she could take in the countryside. The ditches on either side of the road were overgrown with grass and weeds and wildflowers. There were huge yellow daisies with soft brown centers, clumps of lilies and white, lacy-looking flowers she'd never seen before. Even the telephone poles were covered with lush green vines and orange, trumpet-shaped flowers.

She glided past fields of tall corn, their tidy rows neatly following the lay of the land. Some fenced areas had been left as pasture, the rolling green hills dotted with grazing sheep and cattle. Occasionally, among the stands of huge maples and oaks, she would catch a glimpse of a white farmhouse or a red barn. So calm, serene. So homey. Like a Grandma Moses painting.

Suddenly, Jenny's leisurely outing came to a jarring halt in a flapping of old rubber and a skidding of dust.

She managed to catch herself as the bike lurched to a halt. Straddling the frame, feet planted firmly on the ground, Jenny looked down at the split tire, then up at the deserted country road.

Heat waves shimmered above puddle mirages. A trail of sweat trickled down the side of her face, and she swiped at it with the back of her hand. Now that she'd stopped, she realized just how oppressive the day was; she could feel the sun's rays burning through the back of her shirt, feel her dark hair absorbing the fiery heat. A bird flew overhead, silhouetted against the cloudless sky. A monarch butterfly hovered not far from her, then fluttered to a nearby daisy.

Jenny blew out a breath. She had probably come about a mile, which put her about halfway to town. There was nothing to do but turn around and walk the bike home.

She was swinging it around when dust rising above a distant cornfield caught her eye. Someone was coming.

She watched as the cloud moved closer, the long trail making her think of a Roadrunner cartoon, the way it clung to the ground, barely dissipating in the heavy air.

Finally, an old red pickup truck crested the hill, slowed, then came to jerking halt not far from her. The engine was cut, the door squeaked open, and Lucas Tate, dressed in faded jeans and a white T-shirt, stepped out.

He leaned his arms on the upper frame of the open door, one foot inside the truck. His blue eyes went from her face to the bike to the flat, then back again. She could feel the flush steal through her cheeks, feel the tendrils of damp hair sticking to her neck, feel her shirt clinging to her skin, feel him taking careful note of all those things.

Jenny's heart began to hammer, and her palms felt slippery against the bike's handlebars. She squared her shoulders and lifted her chin higher, forcing her eyes to make direct contact with his.

He sauntered to the front of the truck and leaned a hip against the grill, crossing his arms over his chest, biceps bulging. With the toe of one dusty boot, he pushed at a sharp-edged rock. "Gravel's hell on tires."

One corner of his mouth slanted up, and with a jolt, she realized she was staring at his lips. Her eyes darted away, searching for a place to focus, finally settling on the split tire.

Now that she wasn't looking at him, her pulse slowed and she let out a tight breath. "The tires are old."

She thought about how nicely the ride had begun, how she'd hoped the tires would hold air. Her voice dropped, became wistful. "I just hadn't been on a bike in so long." She pressed her lips together, wondering why she'd said that, why she had revealed that much of herself to him.

Without comment, he strode over, picked up the bicycle and swung it up into the bed of the truck. "Hop in and I'll give you a lift back to the house."

"If you could just drop off the bike, I'd appreciate it." She motioned up the road. "I'm going into Ellison for some groceries." She refused to look in his direction. Instead she kept her eyes focused on the nearby cornfield, watching a pair of black birds with red patches on their wings. She'd had a lot of practice shutting people out, keeping them at arm's length.

"Get in the truck and I'll take you."

He didn't ask; he commanded. Jenny had always been slow to anger, but this man seemed to have an uncanny knack for stirring up the dormant emotions in her.

"I may be staying in your grandmother's house, but that doesn't mean you can tell me what to do." Her reaction was childish, but she couldn't help it. She looked at him defiantly. "Thanks, anyway." She turned and started walking.

A door slammed, a motor rumbled to life, tires crunched over gravel. The truck, with Lucas Tate inside, was coasting along beside her. She ignored him and stared straight ahead, hardly noticing the butterflies or the wildflowers any longer.

"Hot, isn't it?" came his conversational voice from the truck. "Forecast says we might hit a hundred today."

She looked over her shoulder. Luke's left arm rested on the top of the steering wheel, neck craned so he could watch her though the open passenger window.

"There's a livestock warning out," he told her.

"Lucky for me I don't have any livestock."

He stayed even with her, motor idling roughly. "There's a pond behind my house you might want to cool off in. And don't worry—I've had basic lifesaving." The teasing glint in his eyes couldn't be missed.

"I'll have to pass."

"The way you're sweating, I'd say there's a good chance you'll be dehydrated before you even get to Ellison."

She stopped, wondering which was louder, her grinding teeth or the truck's grinding gears.

He stopped and she glared at him through the open window.

He zapped her with a dazzling smile.

Her heart fluttered.

Then the sound of an approaching car penetrated Jenny's bemused brain. She tore her eyes from Lucas Tate to catch a flash of metallic blue before the vehicle disappeared behind a rolling hill. She prayed that it contained some sweet old person who would give her a ride, rescue her from this uncomfortable situation.

"Ah, here comes Mason Wilson," Luke drawled. "Ol' Mace is pushing forty but thinks he's sixteen. If I were you, I'd hide. If he sees you, he'll be howling outside your window every night just like a tomcat. He'll phone you every hour of the day."

Jenny watched as a trail of dust rose behind the cornfield, moving toward them at an alarming rate of speed.

"At least get out of the road. What Mason gains in speed, he makes up for in lack of control. Yeah," Luke said with exaggerated thoughtfulness, "I remember when Mason had a crush on Luetta Smith. She was only fifteen. He was twenty-two and fresh out of prison. To impress her, he stole a car and drove by her house all day long, flicking open his switchblade. County sheriff finally hauled him in."

The blue car appeared then disappeared, now only about a quarter of a mile away. Deciding that Lucas Tate might be the lesser of two evils, Jenny groped for the latch on the slowly rolling truck, pressed the button and tugged. The door wouldn't open.

The truck jerked to a halt. "You'll have to either crawl through the window or come around to this side," Luke informed her casually.

She gave the door one last tug, then hurried around to his side. He stepped out and she scooted under the steering wheel across the hot vinyl seat, but only halfway; the rest of the seat was full of veterinary supplies and what appeared to be dirty laundry.

Luke jumped in beside her, slamming the door, his hard muscular body wedged up against hers from waist to knee. She tried to squirm away, but there wasn't room. Her right hip was pressed against a metal toolbox.

The blue car swung around a corner, went into a fishtail, finally straightened, then roared past. Jenny caught a quick glimpse of a gaudy shirt, big teeth and wild hair, a red garter belt hanging from the rearview mirror and two fingers giving them the peace sign. Then Mason was gone, leaving only his choking dust behind him, drifting in the open window.

"Rain," Luke stated, pulling out the emergency brake and putting in the clutch. "Sure could use some rain."

Jenny was sitting with her feet together on the hot floorboards, her hands clasped over her knees. "If you could just drop me off in Ellison, I'd appreciate it."

Luke looked down at her. Her face was partially hidden from him by the lock of shiny hair that brushed her flushed cheek. He inhaled, breathing in the clean scent of her smooth skin, remembering it, liking it. Almost as much as he was liking the way her body felt pressed against him. Then he saw the bruises on her collarbone where the neck of her shirt had fallen open.

"How'd you get this?" He reached out to touch her.

She clutched her collar together and shrank away. "It's nothing."

"Nothing? That's not the kind of bruise you get from a little bump."

"I bruise easily, that's all," she said distantly, staring straight ahead through the dusty windshield.

To Luke it felt as if a door had been firmly closed in his face, as if she'd tucked a part of herself away, safe and inaccessible.

Before he could dwell on it, the CB radio squawked and Jenny jerked, her reaction to the sudden noise seeming unusually acute to Luke. A woman's car-splitting voice came from the black speaker. "Calling Mobile Unit One."

Luke picked up the mike and pressed the switch. "What's up, Jeanie?"

"Lucas. You've got a call at Newt's place."

"On my way." Luke jammed down the mike, then pulled a quick U-turn in the narrow road, leaving a trail of dust equal to Mason's.

Chapter Four

The last thing Jenny wanted to do was accompany Lucas Tate on his veterinary call, but she'd been left no choice in the matter, tucked as she was between him, a bunch of junk and a door that didn't work.

They turned down a heavily shaded, overgrown lane. Branches scraped the sides of the truck as they bounced along. Weeds and grass hit the front grill then vanished to rub loudly underneath the floorboards while tattered leaves were ripped from green limbs and fell inside the truck cab.

Five minutes later, they pulled into a large glen, in the center of which stood a ramshackle gray shingle-sided house surrounded by an amazing tangle of brush. Saplings had sprung up in rusty fence rows, in the crumbled walk, even along the house's stone foundation.

"Newt doesn't believe in lawnmowers," Luke said, pulling the truck to a halt not far from the house.

Obviously he didn't believe in hauling anything to the dump either, Jenny thought to herself. Partially concealed among the weeds and wildflowers—so much so that they almost seemed a natural, if surrealistic part of their surroundings—were two cars, a wringer washing machine, a couple of plows and a rusty tractor. But the oddest thing of all was the cats. Jenny had never seen so many cats. They were everywhere. Lounging along the railings of the rickety porch, under shrubs, under trees . . .

"I think I may have read about this place in a Dr. Seuss book," she said in amazement.

Luke laughed as he stepped from the truck. "Yeah, I always figured this is what cat heaven must look like." He stood with the door open. "Aren't you coming?"

"No, I'll wait here."

He leaned forward, one hand on the door frame, the other on the door. "You can't live around here without meeting your neighbors. Especially Newt."

Jenny didn't know why Luke seemed to be unbending toward her, but it made her suspicious. In no way was she ready to trust him, she sternly told herself as she slid across the seat and out of the truck.

A door slammed and a thin, stoop-shouldered old man in an antiquated black suit hurried down the porch steps to meet them, several cats bounding after him, tails straight up. "It's Sassafras," the man said, wringing his hands, his face open and worried, taking in both Jenny and Luke. "First I thought Sas was just sleepin' like cats do. She likes to sleep in front of the stove," he quickly explained to Jenny, apparently too agitated to register surprise at having a perfect stranger show up with his veterinarian. He turned back to Luke. "But she wouldn't wake up." His voice quavered.

"You say she's inside?" Luke asked.

"On her favorite rug."

"Wait out here and I'll check on her." Luke ran up the steps and disappeared into the house.

"I dearly love all my cats," Newt told Jenny, "but Sassafras is special." His eyes were misty, full of an intense sadness, as if he were begging her to assure him that everything would be okay. "She's my only house kitty. Every morning, right at six, she jumps on the bed and wakes me up."

Jenny felt a tightness in her throat, and her eyes burned. Tears were contagious. Sadness was contagious.

She cast a glance around, wondering what to say, wondering what words of comfort she could offer this poor man. She couldn't think of anything.

A yellow striped kitten crawled over the tip of Newt's black workshoe. With a movement that was spry for such an old man, Newt bent and picked up the cat, cradling it to the front of his disheveled suit.

Then Luke was heading toward them, slowly this time, his expression sober.

Newt saw it and heaved a dejected sigh. "You don't have to tell me, Lucas. Ol' Sas is dead. Guess I knew it. Just didn't want to believe it, that's all. Just hard to imagine every day without—" His words broke off.

"I'm sorry, Newt," Luke said hoarsely.

Newt patted the kitten's head, then put the animal down on the ground. "Guess I'll go get a shovel."

"No, I'll do it," Luke told him. "I know where. Why don't you stay here with Jenny?"

The old man pressed his lips together, then turned his face away and nodded. Luke reached out and gave his shoulder a squeeze before taking off through the tangled grass, leaving Jenny alone with Newt.

The ache in Jenny's throat was worse. She swallowed and let her gaze pan the yard. Tears had always come too easily for her.

When Jenny was little, every small tragedy, whether fiction or nonfiction, had made her sad, made her cry. Her mother had accused her of being emotional to the point of instability, told her that she should face reality and her own problems, not the problems of others, of strangers—and certainly not of people who weren't even real. When Jenny had become a little older and wiser she realized that not everyone had compassion in them, and that one of those people who didn't was Sancha May. Jenny was certain that if her mother were here right now, she would no doubt remind her that she didn't know this man, that his sorrow wasn't her sorrow.

"A lot of my cats used to be wild," Newt suddenly said. "In the winter, when it's biting cold and snow is covering the ground, wild cats show up at my door and I feed them. They have a hard time catching mice when snow's covering everything. But little by little, they get tamer, come closer."

Small talk.

Jenny understood that there was a measure of comfort to be derived from small talk. It gave people something to focus their attention on while they regained control of their emotions.

Pretty soon she was telling Newt about the cat she'd seen last night. He asked what it had looked like, thinking he might have seen it around. By the time Luke came back, the conversation had turned to gardens and crop rotation and Jenny had learned that corn robs soil of nitrogen and beans put it back in.

Luke ran his fingers through his hair, letting out a sound of frustration.

"Not your fault, Luke," Newt told him. "Sas was old. But it sure won't seem the same around here without her."

"No, it won't." Luke said quietly. "It sure won't."

"Had her a long time. Since you were just a boy."

"That's right."

Newt's eyes became distant as he focused on some memory from the past. "Remember how you'd come by here for milk and cookies after school? You'd sit at the table and Sassafras would lie across your shoulders while you ate."

"I remember."

A heavy silence descended.

Luke decided he needed a cigarette in a bad way. It had been three months since he'd quit smoking, but at times like these—times of emotional stress—the craving came back, strong as ever. He felt his T-shirt pocket for the tongue depressors he kept on hand to chew on whenever he got the urge to smoke. No tongue depressors. He'd have to tough this one out without them.

Situations like this were hard on him—not just on his attempt to overcome his nicotine addiction, but on his heart. Even though Luke dealt with life and death every day, he'd never gotten used to it.

Since the age of twelve, Luke had known he wanted to become a veterinarian. But he'd only thought about saving animals, easing their suffering, fighting cruelty. He hadn't really thought about having to deal one on one with the owners of the animals that didn't make it.

And that part was the hardest for him to handle. Probably because he had such a soft spot for old people and kids. The problem was that old people usually had old pets. And old pets die. Kids had young pets, but young pets, especially dogs, weren't smart. They hadn't learned that those black tires that are so much fun to chase can hurt like hell when they roll over you. And young cats don't know that climbing into a car engine to get warm is a bad idea. Animals, just like most people, get wiser with age. If they manage to live that long.

Old people and kids....

A group of kittens was tumbling and playing together under a peony bush. Luke went over and scooped up the homeliest one of the bunch, holding a hand under its belly, his other hand supporting its tiny, clawed feet. He lifted it high enough to peer into its face. "Look here, Newt. This fella looks a little like ol' Sas."

Wrenched from his deep thoughts, Newt trained his eyes on the kitten. "What do you know—it does at that. I never noticed it before." He took the animal from Luke. "Even has the dark spot on its nose."

Luke picked up another of the kittens, checking to see if its eyes were clear and its skin in good condition. "About time for distemper shots again," he said. "What do you say I stop by tomorrow and we'll do the whole tribe?"

Jenny wondered how in the world they went about vaccinating so many cats at one time. How could they keep track of them all?

"Since you're already here, how 'bout doing them right now?" Newt asked. "Then you won't have to make a special trip." The last words were hastily tacked on, and Jenny suspected that Newt didn't want to be alone.

Luke turned to Jenny. "Are you in a hurry? Would you like to help with a cat roundup?"

She smiled at his choice of words. "I'd love to help."

And so Jenny found out how they managed to vaccinate so many cats.

Newt scurried around the yard, catching cats, one at a time. He brought them to Luke while Jenny sat cross-legged on the ground, filling the syringe with two cc's of vaccine before passing it to Luke.

Before giving them the shot, Luke patiently examined each animal as if he had all the time in the world, keeping his voice low. When he was done giving the vaccination, he marked the finished cat on the back with an orange grease stick, which he'd earlier explained was normally used for marking livestock.

As Jenny helped, she realized she was seeing a totally different side of Lucas Tate. Kneeling in the grass, head bent, disheveled hair lying over his ears as he cradled a tiny kitten in his gentle hands, Luke's love of animals was apparent. And as Jenny watched him with the cats, a bittersweet warmth seeped through her veins, and the tightness that seemed to be so much a part of her now relaxed.

It appeared that Stella was right about her grandson. Right now, Luke certainly looked every inch an "ornery rapscallion with a soft heart." And when Jenny really thought about it, who would blame him for reacting—or overreacting—the way he had the day they'd met? He'd been thinking of his grandmother, looking out for her.

"That's the last one," Newt announced an hour later.

"I know we missed a few—the ones that are mousing," Luke said. "I'll stop by tonight and get them."

"Just be sure and send me a bill this time," Newt said.

"How about a game of checkers and a bottle of dandelion wine in exchange for services rendered?"

"Vaccine don't come cheap, even for a vet—"

"Okay, throw in supper tonight, and we'll call it even."

Newt smiled and nodded. "You're on."

As Luke and Jenny drove away, Jenny took one last look at Newt's home, hardly noticing the junk, seeing instead the differently colored cats dotted among the green, like wildflowers. Newt held up a hand in farewell and she waved back.

Luke pulled out of the shady, rutted lane onto the gravel road. As the truck picked up speed, hot wind rushed in the open windows, whipping Jenny's hair around, sending the sweet scent of it teasing toward him. He became especially aware of the way her warm body was pressed against his. He could feel the dampness of her skin where their arms touched. It would be nice to feel more of her skin pressed to his, he decided.

In Ellison, while Jenny did her grocery shopping, Luke visited the feed store adjacent to Ellison General Store. When she came out, he was surprised to find that the only purchase she'd made was a bag of cat food.

Fifteen minutes later, they were pulling up in front of Jenny's house. Luke jerked on the emergency brake and hopped from the truck, Jenny scooting across the seat after him. As soon as her foot touched the ground, he quickly pulled her toward him, steadying her with both hands. "Careful," he warned, nodding toward the place where she'd almost stepped. "Leaves of three, let it be."

She looked down at the shiny, three-leafed plant near her foot, then back up at him, suspicion in her eyes. "I'm wearing jeans."

He shrugged. "Doesn't always matter. Poison ivy gets on your shoes, then you take them off, get it on your hands. The rest is history."

The suspicion faded from her brown eyes. "I'll remember that."

He realized he was still holding her arms. Reluctantly he let go, then stood there, waiting, not wanting her to go inside. He tried to think of something else to say so she wouldn't leave.

"My bike is in your truck," she reminded him.

"Oh, yeah."

Funny thing was, the bike belonged to him. In eighth grade, Luke had chopped a lot of wood to pay for that bike. But if Jenny knew it was his, she wouldn't use it. He was sure of that. "I have a friend, Danny Talbot—he owns the gas station in Ellison.

Why don't I drop the bike off there, have him take a look at the tires?"

Indecision flitted across her face.

"It's the least I can do for all your help. You're a good assistant. Last time we vaccinated Newt's cats, it took the two of us about three hours."

"I've never done anything like that before. It was fun."

"You've surely taken a cat to the vet for shots sometime in your life."

She shook her head and the smile, when it came, seemed wistful. "It would be nice if you'd drop off the bike for me." Then she turned, and as she walked up the green, sloping yard to the house there was an aloneness about her, as if she'd wrapped herself in a cloak of solitude.

After she'd gone inside, Luke stood a while longer, hands jammed into the front pockets of his jeans, staring at the front door.

He thought about how she'd drawn away from him earlier when he'd asked about the bruise. It had seemed as if a door had been firmly closed. Luke had seen that withdrawal, that pulling away somewhere before...

Then it came to him. Danny. Danny had acted like that after getting back from Vietnam.

Chapter Five

Saturday morning dawned hot and sultry. The dispirited mood that always lurked in the shadows of Jenny's nightmare weighed heavy upon her, seeming to cast a spell, cursing her with depression and fatigue before she could even get out of bed to start the day.

In her sleep she couldn't fight it, but now that she was awake her conscious mind kicked in, tearing at the cobwebs left in her psyche by the faceless dream.

From downstairs the phone shrilled, and Jenny's heart knocked in her chest. She swung her feet to the floor, joints popping, body aching. Her white chemise nightgown brushed against slim calves as she made her way down the stairs to the kitchen, catching the phone on the fifth ring.

"Jenny, dear. I hope I didn't wake you," came Stella's voice crackling across the antiquated phone lines.

Jenny pushed limp strands of hair back from her face, willing her galloping heartbeat to slow, trying to focus her thoughts. Thankfully the dark mood induced by the dream was lifting, becoming just a sense of vague discomfort in the back of her mind.

"I'm calling about the county fair," Stella said. "You must come with me today. Saturday's the biggest day and everybody will be there."

"County fair?" Jenny reached out, pulled one of the slat-backed chairs across the linoleum and sat down, crossing her legs at the knees. "I don't know, Stella..."

Jenny had never been to a county fair, but she'd seen the movie *State Fair* and had a sudden memory of an actor singing to his pig.

"Of course you'll come," Stella insisted in the no-nonsense voice sometimes employed by women her age, a voice that meant: I've lived longer, I know more, so it stands to reason I'm right.

"I didn't invite you here so you could become a hermit," Stella said. "I know you've had a hard time and are trying to forget about what happened in Mexico, but keeping to yourself won't help. It's not good for a body to be alone all the time."

Jenny knew Stella was right, yet the thought of having to meet people, having to bump shoulders with strangers in a crowd didn't appeal to her at all.

With a start, Jenny realized Stella was still talking.

"...you'll have to fix something for a picnic, and be sure to make it for two. If I remember right, there's a basket in the cupboard above the icebox."

"Picnic?"

"Don't fret over it. It doesn't have to be anything fancy." There was a thoughtful pause. "Course Myra Locks will most likely have her special fried chicken. Probably deviled eggs and apple pie." Stella gave a derisive snort. "But that's only because she's getting long in the tooth and is cooking out of sheer desperation."

Jenny hadn't the vaguest notion what Stella was talking about. She must have missed an important part of the conversation, but she didn't want to hurt the older woman's feelings by admitting that her mind had drifted.

Stella wouldn't have to know that Jenny hadn't been hanging on her every word, she decided, because she wasn't going to the fair anyway. She took a breath, intending to politely decline.

"I'll be over to get you about two o'clock. And don't forget the picnic basket," Stella barked with finality.

Click.

Jenny sat with the humming receiver in her hand. She could call her back, but she had the feeling Stella wouldn't listen to any amount of protestation. Jenny sighed. At the moment, she could almost sympathize with Lucas Tate. His grandmother was a domineering, manipulative woman . . . who was motivated by kindness. Stella could be irritating, yes, but she could be oh, so endearing.

Jenny smiled and hung up the receiver.

A county fair . . . and a picnic . . .

She'd never been to a county fair, never been on a picnic. Maybe it wouldn't be so bad. Maybe it would even be fun. . . .

When Stella's old black gangster car crept up the gravel drive, Jenny was waiting on the porch wearing her favorite jeans, hair tied back with a pastel ribbon that went with her floral-print camp shirt, wicker basket handle clutched in both hands.

It turned out that the fairgrounds were located on the outskirts of Ellison in a level pasture edged by huge oak trees.

Even with a pillow at her back, Stella had to crane her neck to see over the dashboard and point the toe of her black shoe to reach the gas pedal. Nevertheless she was somehow able to maintain a sort of regal aplomb as she guided the big car through the propped-open wooden gate, then wrestled with the steering wheel until she finally managed to maneuver the vehicle into the field, parking alongside a truck and livestock trailer.

That feat accomplished, Stella turned off the ignition, reminded Jenny about the picnic basket and stepped from the car, shutting the long, heavy door with both hands.

Stella had exercised a great deal more restraint in dressing than usual today, Jenny noticed. She'd even left her boa at home. Jenny marveled at how she managed to look so fresh and cool, clothed as she was in a long-sleeved black silk dress with a fragile pin lace collar.

"The grounds take up all of ten acres," Stella informed her as they picked their way across the alfalfa stubble.

Jenny had no idea how much an acre was, but she guessed that the pasture would cover a couple of city blocks. Huge, green-striped canvas tents stood festively among corrugated aluminum roofs and penned lots. To one side was a dirt arena with wooden bleachers. At one end, atop poles, stood a judge's booth complete with PA system. To the left of all this was the carnival. She could see a ferris wheel turning above the tent tops. Sounds of milling livestock and distorted rock music drifted toward them along with the mingled smells of popcorn and hot dogs, diesel exhaust and cotton candy.

The first thing they did was to go to the Home Ec building so the picnic basket could be dropped off and tagged.

"It's a raffle," Stella explained to Jenny as the woman at the counter attached a pink slip of paper to the basket, then handed the other half to Jenny.

"We don't eat our own lunches?" Jenny asked in sudden alarm, thinking of the pitiful meal she'd thrown together. She wasn't even sure peanut butter sandwiches and lemon Kool-Aid qualified as a meal.

"What a silly notion. Why of course you eat your own food." Stella reached out and gave her a reassuring pat on the hand. "Don't worry about a thing."

They stood in the wide doorway of the Home Ec building, trying to decide whether to watch the log-splitting contest or the water witching demonstration, when a deep voice carried through a tightly grouped throng of people, drawing both their attention.

"Why, that's Luke," Stella said, standing on tiptoe, trying to see around the crowd.

Jenny was surprised to find that she, too, had recognized Luke's voice. But then, she argued to herself, there was a distinctiveness about it, a hint of an accent that made Lucas Tate's voice hard to mistake for anyone else's. The accent didn't sound regional. No, it was more like something that came from Luke himself. There was a sensual, laid-back quality to his speech pattern, especially the way he pronounced his O's, with an almost Canadian lilt.

"Come on, Danny!" came Luke's voice, carrying through the semicircle of people. "You know what your problem is? You've been spending too much time sitting around playing cards, waiting for that gas station bell to ring. Your pitching arm's gone weak!"

Stella laid a hand on Jenny's arm. "When I told Luke we were coming here, he got riled and said he didn't want to see either of us poking our noses around the fairgrounds this afternoon. Told me to stay clean

away from here till evening. Can you imagine a
grandson telling his own grandmother to stay clean
away? I never. Made me want to give his ear a good
tug." She looked at Jenny and her blue eyes suddenly
danced with mischief—a telltale sign of just where
Luke had come by the flash of devilment that had lit
his eyes on more than one occasion.

"So I just naturally had to come and see what he
was up to," Stella said.

Jenny smiled back, her own curiosity aroused. She
spotted an opening in the crowd and motioned for
Stella to follow.

They cut through the alleyway of people, stopping
at the edge. A gasp of laughter escaped Jenny before
she clapped a hand to her mouth.

Perched in an orange and white dunk tank was Lucas Tate, with a sign above him that read: Three
Throws for a Dollar. All Proceeds Benefit the Humane Society.

Stella leaned toward Jenny. "I used to threaten to
lock him in a cage, but never did it," she commented
dryly. "Looks good on him, don't it?" Some of the
people nearest them turned and laughed good-
naturedly.

"Mmmm." Jenny had to agree. He did indeed look
good. The only clothing he wore was a pair of ragged
cutoffs. So far, no one had hit the metal target that
released the seat, dumping the occupant of the tank
into four feet of chilly water. Luke was still dry. And
tanned. He was very tan—every well-formed muscle,

every taut bicep and lean, hard limb that was exposed
to her eyes...

She suddenly realized she was all but ogling him.
Hot confusion rose in her cheeks. What on earth was
the matter with her? Her gaze swept the ground, the
sky, the crowd, then flashed back to Luke.

Fingers locked in the side grillwork of the cage, bare
feet swinging, Luke kept up a steady string of banter
any well-versed carny would envy. "One last try,
Danny boy!"

Luckily, with his laughter-creased eyes focused on
the stocky man who had paid for a chance to knock
him in the water, he hadn't noticed Stella or Jenny yet.

Danny took a sideways pitcher's stance, bent both
knees, adjusted his green cap, then wound up, releas-
ing on the outward swing of his arm. The ball missed
the metal lever and fell with a harmless thud against
the canvas backdrop. The crowd let out a unanimous,
disappointed sigh.

"Thought you had him that time," a bystander
commented.

"Better hang up the baseball bat and pick up some
knitting needles, Danny!" Luke taunted.

The man who had thrown the ball laughed. "I never
could send a ball into the strike zone when that tongue
of yours was flappin'."

"Tell you what. Put another buck down and I'll
keep my mouth—" Luke broke off. He had spotted
Jenny and Stella.

For a fraction of a second, Jenny thought he looked almost embarrassed, but that fleeting expression quickly changed to one Jenny had no difficulty interpreting as irritation—irritation at finding that his grandmother had done exactly what he'd asked her not to.

"What a surprise," he drawled loudly. "If it isn't my grandmother, accompanied by Miss May. I do declare."

Luke's booming voice had to be carrying across the entire fairgrounds. People were turning to stare and Jenny felt like crawling under the nearest rock.

Stella leaned close and whispered to Jenny. "Luke must have gotten a good night's sleep. He's feeling feisty."

Jenny was about to say that his reaction probably had something to do with their presence here, when he threw out another taunt. "Yes siree, bob! Don't know when I've seen you look lovelier, Miss May! Care to take a shot at me? It's for a worthy cause. As the sign says—" he pointed "—proceeds go to the Humane Society."

Why had he singled her out, Jenny wondered. Did he think she'd encouraged Stella to come? Or did he think he was safe in assuming that she couldn't hit the target? Well, she'd show him differently.

Jenny pulled a dollar bill from the back pocket of her jeans, stepped forward and stuffed it through the slitted lid of the coffee can. Then she picked up a ball, making a show of testing it, tossing it gently in the air.

"Uh-oh, Lucas. Looks like you might be in trouble," the man named Danny said, laughing.

Luke flicked his hand, as if to wave the words away. "I don't think I have anything to worry about. She probably throws like you."

Jenny rubbed her palm down the front of her denim pant leg while Luke calmly waited, his expression making her think of the way an adult might watch a child attempting something totally beyond his capabilities. She took careful aim, then tossed the ball, just missing the round metal target.

"Shoot!" she muttered, disgusted with herself. Her pitching was rusty.

"What'd I tell you?" Luke drawled. "Throws like a girl. Maybe you better step up here to the kiddie line, sweetheart."

"No thanks." Jenny was grimly determined now. She'd knock him in the water if it took her life savings—which actually, when she thought about it, wasn't a whole lot.

"Come on, Jenny girl," Stella encouraged from the sidelines. "Give that grandson of mine a good dunking. He needs it."

Jenny walked up to the cage and picked up two balls. She couldn't help glancing over her shoulder at Luke. He flashed her a grin, then leaned closer. "If I were you, I'd quit while I was ahead. Save yourself the embarrassment of two more sissie throws."

"I'm surprised girls aren't fighting each other for the chance to dunk you—if you sweet talk them the way you sweet talk me."

"They fight over me, all right." He let out a gusty sigh. "But I don't think dunking is what they have in mind."

"Good grief." The man was impossible.

"Quit your talkin'," Danny shouted. "I want to see you get dunked."

Jenny looked directly into Luke's clear eyes and smiled. "Me, too." Then she marched back to the line. With the toe of her tennis shoe, she found an indentation in the ground that felt just right and balanced her weight.

She aimed.

He taunted. "Never in a million years."

She tossed.

There was a clunk of metal, a look of comical dismay on Luke's face, followed by a loud yelp and a huge splash. The audience roared their approval.

"Good girl!" Stella yelled.

"'Bout time you had an all-over bath," Danny shouted through cupped hands.

"I always said the boy might not look half-bad with a haircut and a good scrubbing," joked an old timer.

Luke came up sputtering, water sloshing over the sides of the tank. "A fluke," he gasped, water streaming down his face, down his hard body. "A mere fluke." He turned to fix the seat, then levered himself back up with deceptive ease.

Jenny was poised to toss the next ball when she allowed her eyes to stray from the target to Luke. Her breath caught and she faltered, her insides feeling strange, weak . . .

That's when it occurred to her that Lucas Tate looked even better wet than dry. His hard muscles gleamed slickly in the summer sun; his dark hair was plastered to a broad chest; his eyelashes were black, wet spikes set around the startling turquoise of his eyes.

He brought up both hands and raked the hair back from his face, water sluicing down his neck and running in rivulets around his shoulders. Then he clasped his hands together between his knees and settled himself down to wait. "You'll never be able to do it again," he said smugly, never seeming to consider the possibility that she might actually be able to throw.

And it was that very smugness that brought Jenny back around. "I used to be on the Beachcomber's womens' fast pitch team," she informed him matter-of-factly.

"Oh?" An oh-so-tolerant smile. "What were you? Water girl?"

"No." She wound up, released the ball and a cocky Lucas Tate splashed from his perch for the second time, surfacing to glare at her through streaming water and plastered-down hair.

Jenny gave him a sweet smile. "Pitcher."

Jenny amd Stella spent the rest of the afternoon leisurely strolling across clipped, sweet smelling grass,
admiring colorful handmade quilts and rugs along
with an array of blue ribbon pies and jellies. Jenny was
introduced to several people and even though she was
aware that most of them had probably already passed
her name back and forth across the kitchen table along
with the cream and sugar, she didn't really mind because they seemed genuinely kind and eager to meet
her.

As she and Stella wandered through the crowd, the
shimmering sun getting lower and larger in the summer sky, snatches of conversation drifted hazily toward them.

". . . uncommonly hot weather."

"Yep. Dog days."

"Jet streams. Heat's caused by them airplanes
flying overhead, making them danged jet streams."

"...dog was dead three days 'fore Myrtle called the
vet. Told Luke ol' Shep appeared to be feelin' a mite
under the weather."

Wheezing, braying laughter.

"Maybe that's why they call 'em dog days."

More laughter.

Jenny smiled, feeling herself relax, feeling herself
being lulled by the heat and the lazy atmosphere.

Stella looked at her silver watch and announced that
it was almost five o'clock; time to get to the game tent.

When they arrived, they found the tent almost full
and all the seats at the long cafeteria tables taken. That

was okay, though. They decided it would be cooler to stand on the sidelines where the tent's canvas walls had been rolled up and secured to take advantage of the breeze that was picking up.

Stella pointed her chin in the direction of the stage that stood at one end of the tent. "I see Boone Bailey's running things again this year. He's the fella I was telling you about the other day—the one who brings me those wonderful furs."

Standing on the stage in front of a floor microphone was a person who looked the perfect counterpart to Stella Tate. A small, wiry man, Boone Bailey was wearing dark trousers and a semitransparent V-neck T-shirt with a bolo tie. This ensemble was topped off with a black, flat-brimmed Spanish style hat complete with chin string.

Jenny was fast coming to realize that Stella wasn't the only eccentric in the area. In fact, it almost seemed that Ellison bred colorful people. And Jenny had to wonder about all the TV ads that portrayed rural midwesterners as dull and ordinary. The people who made those ads had obviously never been to Ellison, Iowa.

"What's he getting ready to do?" Jenny whispered to Stella.

"Raffle. The single men draw raffle tickets to see who wins what basket," Stella said without a flicker of an eyelid, not a glimmer of guilt.

Now Jenny noticed the picnic baskets lined up on a long table that stood to the left of Mr. Bailey. "You said we eat our own lunch." Jenny found it hard to keep her voice level.

"Oh, you do eat your own lunch," Stella said, eyes focused on the man on the stage. "You eat it with whoever wins your basket. And whoever wins you," she added almost as an afterthought.

Good grief.

Jenny felt as if the Women's Movement had just taken a giant step backwards—into a whole other century. "Why, that's . . . that's archaic!"

Her mind raced. Maybe she could get her basket back before things got underway. Maybe she could just casually walk up and snatch it from the table.

"Oh, pooh!" Stella scoffed, delicately flicking a blue-veined hand. "It's all in fun. Been doing it for the last fifty years. In honor of Ellison's founder, Banjo Ellison. He won his wife in a poker game."

Jenny's heart fell somewhere around the region of her stomach, and she began to wonder if maybe Stella wasn't a little mad, if maybe the whole town of Ellison wasn't a little mad. She remembered a saying she'd once heard: everyone is crazy except for thee and me, and sometimes I wonder about thee.

"Story goes that Banjo won her from a French trader who claimed she knew how to cook like nobody's business. Turned out she could barely stoke a stove and didn't know a speck of English. But apparently that didn't bother Banjo, 'cause they wound up having ten kids."

Not a reassuring story by any means, Jenny thought glumly.

"Ladies and gentlemen and children of all ages," Boone announced in a deep, dramatic, ringmaster's voice. The microphone let out an earsplitting squawk. Adults groaned and children clapped small hands to their ears.

Boone dragged the mike stand a few feet away from the speaker, stopping the feedback. "Now for the event all Ellison's been waiting for—the event renowned for bringing together couples who might otherwise be two ships passing in the night. The event that brought about the wedded bliss of Danny Talbot and his fair P.J., the event that brought about the blackened eye and bruised shin of Mike Dougherty." He struck an evangelist's open-armed pose. "Welcome one and all to the Forty-ninth Annual Picnic Basket Raffle! Will all the participating bachelors please step up to the stage?"

There was a shuffling of feet, and then several men came forward.

Jenny's heart sank another notch: Lucas Tate was among them. He'd changed out of his wet clothes and was now wearing jeans and a yellow T-shirt that said Animals Are Kind to Dumb People.

Stella leaned close. "Lucas hates doing this, but he's on the fair committee, so he has no choice." She giggled like a young girl.

Jenny could only frantically wonder how this had happened, how she had gotten herself into such a situation.

A two syllable noun was the answer to her question. *Stella.*

With regal gestures, Boone swept off his black felt hat, turned it upside down, dropped the raffle tickets into the crown, stirred them up and held out the hat to the men.

"Now you all know the rules. The raffle tickets are different colors. All you do is match your half of the ticket with the little lady who prepared the picnic and you get the basket and the woman till eight o'clock tonight. Now, if after the meal is consumed, she decides she can't tolerate your company any longer, she can pay five dollars to the fair committee and the blessed union will be dissolved. Oh, and men, I shouldn't have to remind you to mind your manners. This doesn't give you the right to steal any kisses. That is unless the girl's willin'."

There was a roar of approving laughter as the hat was passed and each man picked out a colored slip of paper.

"Oh, my," Stella said quietly. "Oh, dear."

"What?" What else could possibly happen, Jenny wondered.

"Who on earth allowed Mason Wilson to participate? Last year he tossed poor Harriet Marshall over his shoulder and started to leave with her—just like some hillbilly. We had to go after him. Course it was agreed that Harriet didn't have to pay the five dollars for the mock divorce.''

Mason.

Mason was the person with the loud blue car. The one who had passed them on the road yesterday. The one with the long, tangled hair, the peace sign, the red garter belt.

The one with the prison record.

The men were done drawing and Jenny strained to see who held the other half of her ticket. Most of the men gripped their tickets in their palms, so they couldn't be seen, but Mason had the edge of his pinched between two fingers, grinning and waving it in the air. His ticket was pink.

But then, Jenny had never considered herself lucky. She'd never won a door prize, never found a four-leaf clover.

Having to face Lucas Tate after dunking him would have been better than having Mason draw her ticket. Having Luke laugh at her sandwiches would have been better than having to share them with Mason. Lucas Tate made her heart race, but in a totally different way, a scary-exciting way. The thought of having to spend the rest of the day with Mason made her heart race in just plain fear.

"There you go," Boone said. "All you ladies with tickets please stand and hold your colors high so your beau can find you."

Jenny froze. She couldn't make herself reach into the back pocket of her jeans to pull out her piece of paper. She wanted to run, to get away.

She glanced over her shoulder. While she had been watching the stage, people had crowded behind her, closing her in.

Trapping her, like the dream.

Her heart began to constrict. She tried to tell herself not to panic, not to allow the claustrophobia to gain control, but it didn't do any good. The tightness in her chest grew, shortening her breath.

Frantically, her eyes darted around the enclosure, stopping when they locked with Luke's.

He stood on the stage, watching her, an unreadable expression on his face. Then his eyes shifted away.

An intense sense of loss, of abandonment, filled her. She was sickeningly conscious of the tightly-packed people in front of her, of the tightly-packed people behind her, of the packed ground beneath her feet, of the green tent roof pushing down from above.

No way out.

Trapped.

She was trapped. Trapped, trapped, trapped. Like a rat in a cage, a mouse in a maze.

She had to get out of here, she told herself, had to leave.

Turn and walk away. Just turn and walk away.

But she couldn't make herself move, couldn't make her muscles respond to the commands her mind was sending. She bowed her head and squeezed her eyes shut, trying to block out her surroundings, forcing herself to take shallow breaths, to focus on herself instead of the smothering space around her.

"Hey—" The single word came to her, soft and low and edged with concern. Then, "You're not chickening out on me, are you?"

The voice that broke through the flimsy shell she'd mentally constructed was a voice she would have recognized in the darkest dark. Her eyes flew open.

Luke stood in front of her, looking big and solid and strangely enough—safe. She had the almost irrepressible urge to throw herself at his chest and hang on for dear life.

But that wasn't her way. Hiding—that was her way.

There was something in his expression... curiosity...puzzlement? Or was it worry that clouded the ocean-blue of his eyes?

Almost as if relieved, he let out his breath. Then a slow, lazy smile touched the corners of his sensuous mouth. "For a minute, I thought you might be going down for the count."

All she could seem to do was stand there, feeling weak and hot, lost in his eyes, lost in his smile. Then something tickled the end of her nose and she drew back. In Luke's hand was the other half of her ticket.

Chapter Six

Next thing Jenny knew Luke had grabbed her by the arm and was pulling her after him, cutting a path through the throng of people.

As soon as the fresh air and sunshine hit her face the claustrophobic feeling lifted and she could breathe again. Gradually she became aware of the fact that Luke was watching her closely, furrowed lines etched between his sun-tinged brows. She took another stabilizing breath, willing the tension in her to relax.

"How did you manage that?" she finally asked, surprised and thankful to find that her voice still worked and that it sounded so normal. With one hand, she shaded her eyes against the hazy orange glow of the late afternoon sun. "You didn't draw my ticket."

He shrugged, his mouth twisting into a half smile. "Myra's one of the best cooks around. All I had to do was pass that huge basket of hers under Mason's nose and let him get a whiff of her fried chicken. Mason loves fried chicken. When we were in grade school, Mason used to beg to scrape plates on the days we had chicken—in case somebody left a piece."

Luke glanced over his shoulder, then jerked his head in the direction they'd come. "Look there."

Jenny looked. Mason Wilson and Myra Locks were facing off. The couple was too far away for Jenny to hear what the argument was about, but it was obvious they were arguing.

Luke clicked his tongue, then sighed heavily. "A match made in hell."

The dark panic that had so enveloped Jenny was completely gone, almost as if by magic. Now she could barely manage to contain the laughter that threatened to burst from her, guiltily chastising herself for not feeling sorrier for Myra. "She shouldn't have to put up with him on my account."

"Don't worry about Myra. She can handle Mason. And she's too big for him to toss over his shoulder. In fact, I wouldn't be surprised if she tossed *him* over *her* shoulder."

He could be right, Jenny decided. Even though Myra was wearing flats and Mason was wearing black engineer boots, Myra stood inches above him, her sleeveless polyester dress pulled tightly across a broad chest and rib cage.

"I appreciate what you did, but I'm sure you don't want to go through with the rest of this," Jenny said, not wanting Luke to discover that he'd exchanged a sumptuous feast for a peanut butter sandwich. Actually, she couldn't quite understand why he'd come to her rescue at all. Then she thought about the look that had passed between them in the tent—almost telepathic. She had called out for help; he had answered. But that was ridiculous. Totally ridiculous.

She put out her hand to take the basket from him. "If you don't mind, I'll just slip away and nobody will ever know."

"Mind? Are you kidding? You're talking about Ellison, Iowa, where people know everything about everybody right down to the size, color and style of their underwear. Within five minutes everybody will be laughing and talking about how I got dumped at the Forty-ninth Annual Picnic Basket Raffle. Shoot, I wouldn't be surprised if they put on a play about it at the opera house next year. So unless you want to make a laughingstock out of me, we'll have to spend the next couple of hours together."

Jenny hesitated, picturing those two sandwiches that resided so pathetically at the bottom of the basket Luke still held.

"Come on. Don't you think you've embarrassed me enough for the day?" he asked. "Don't you think you owe me one after dunking me like you did?"

"*I've* embarrassed *you*? If you'll remember correctly, you're the one who drew everyone's attention to me!" she fumed. "You're the one who dared me to knock you into that tank of water—and that was only because you didn't think I could do it!"

Jenny clamped her mouth shut, realizing that it was starting again.

She, who was normally a noncombustible person, became highly flammable when combined with the catalyzing presence of Lucas Tate.

"I've got an idea," he said. "What do you say we declare the fairgrounds a demilitarized zone and call a truce for the rest of the day?"

"I don't know if a truce is possible."

"We got along yesterday. There's no reason why we can't get along today. It'll be a cinch—I'll be polite to you, you be polite to me." He put out his hand, waiting for her to come along. "I know this great shady place right by a stream."

An unsettling nervousness ran through her. She didn't know if she was ready for this. Alone with Lucas Tate? A memory came to her: a memory of a kiss, of the way it had made her blood rush through her veins.

"Luke! Luke!"

A young girl of about ten came running across the grass toward them, a white bonnet hanging loosely down her back above a waterfall of flying golden hair. She was pulling a little boy along behind her, his short legs trying to keep up. Both were dressed like Quakers or Amish, or maybe pilgrims, the girl wearing a black dress with a white pinafore, the boy in knickers, white cotton shirt and black suspenders.

They came to a breathless halt a few feet away. Luke set the picnic basket down near his feet and introduced his godchildren, Kelly and Jacob Talbot. "And what have my favorite early settlers been up to?"

The girl wrinkled her freckled nose. "Mom made us wear these funny clothes and help her make apple butter."

"Daddy said our clothes were dapper." Jacob wriggled his hand free of his sister's so he could stand near Luke. "What's dapper mean?"

Kelly was pretty and vivacious, but this child, this sweet little boy with his flushed porcelain cheeks and red rosebud mouth took Jenny's breath away. Huge molasses eyes solemnly watched her from beneath the flat brim of his black hat. Blond hair, damp with perspiration, clung to his neck and forehead.

Luke grinned. "Dapper means you look about as good as a fella can look." He bent down and lifted Jacob, swinging him up to his broad shoulders, settling one small, chubby leg on either side of his neck. "When your daddy was little and would get all gussied up, we called him Dapper Dan."

A flicker of a smile crossed the child's serious features, and Jenny wondered if he was always so sober.

"We're gonna make ice cream," Kelly said. "Daddy had to go help Jake Chapman get his John Deere ready for the tractor pull and Mom wants to know if you'll help turn the crank on the ice cream maker. She said to tell you nobody else turns it as good as you.''

Luke clicked his tongue. ''Flattery, flattery.''

Jacob locked fat chubby fingers together above Luke's eyebrows and settled his small chin on the top of Luke's sun-streaked hair.

''Only if Jacob helps, and only if it's strawberry ice cream.'' Luke looked up. ''Right, Jacob?''

''Right.''

''Prepare for lift-off.'' Luke put his hands on the boy's waist, lifted him free of his shoulders and swung him to the ground.

Jacob came over to Jenny and looked up at her, eyes big. ''You're not going to take Luke away, are you?'' he whispered in a husky voice that tore at her heart.

Her eyes flashed to Luke, but he hadn't heard. He was laughing at something Kelly was telling him. Jenny crouched down in front of Jacob. ''Of course I'm not taking Luke away.'' Where had the child come by such a notion?

Jacob looked down at the ground and shuffled his feet. ''I thought since you and Luke are married now, you'll want him to leave with you like Mom said Cassie wanted.'' His bottom lip trembled. ''I don't want Luke to go away.''

Comprehension came to her. Cassie was the girl Luke almost married—the girl who had refused to live in Ellison. Jenny reached out to take hold of one of Jacob's small, hot hands. ''We're not married. This is only pretend . . . it's only for fun. For the fair.''

"It is?"

"Yes."

She saw the relief wash over him. And then he smiled at her and it was like the sun coming out after a gentle rain. She let go of his hand and stood up.

"Do you like homemade ice cream?" he asked.

"I've never had it, but I'll bet I'd like it."

"Never?" His expression was one of wonder.

"Never."

"Didn't you ever have a mommy?" After the words were out, he instantly looked ashamed, as if remembering that he wasn't supposed to ask people those kinds of questions.

"Well...yes. But not all mommies make homemade ice cream."

He absorbed that information, then turned to Luke. "Jenny's never ate homemade ice cream."

"That a fact? Then we'll have to make sure she has some, won't we?" Luke looked at Jenny. "What do you say? Feel like an ice cream-making detour before our picnic?"

"It sounds like fun," Jenny said truthfully. And it would also delay the opening of her picnic basket. "Lead the way."

The children scampered ahead, with Jenny and Luke following. Jacob's hat blew off, the gust of wind cartwheeling it across the field of sweet clover and dandelions. The sound of laughter floated back to them as the children raced after the hat, Kelly's skirt billowing about her calves.

Watching them, a lightness came to Jenny, and she suddenly knew that this was a very special place, full of special people.

When they reached the Talbots' camper, they found P.J. sitting in a lawn chair, pouring the ice cream mixture into a wooden bucket. With her long, straight strawberry-blond hair she hardly looked much older than Kelly, Luke thought.

P.J. stood up, and from her expression he could tell that she was tickled as all get out to see him with a member of the opposite sex. Ever since Cassie had left, P.J. had considered it her duty to find a soul mate for him. She was always trying to fix him up with somebody. She just couldn't seem to help herself. He'd always figured it was something inborn, like the way Stella had to have the storm windows off her house by the first of April, even if they had to be taken down in the middle of a blizzard. Or the way robins showed up when there was snow on the ground. A case of instinct gone haywire.

P.J. and Jenny seemed to hit it off right away. Talking and laughing, they scooted themselves onto the tailgate of the camper. P.J. had a glint in her eye and he caught her regarding him with what he commonly referred to as her Madame Talbot, Fortune Teller *Extraordinaire* expression. He could even picture her hunched over her crystal ball, turban on her head.

Somewhere in your future I see a girl, a woman... and a ring of gold. Children... I see children. Does any of this mean anything to you?

Luke shook his head and walked over to the ice cream maker, sitting down in the chair P.J. had vacated. "Looks like we need a little more ice," he noted innocently.

Poor choice of words.

Both children dashed to snatch up the plastic bag of melting ice. "I had it first!" Kelly said, tugging.

Jacob was hugging the sweating bag to his chest as if it was his favorite stuffed toy, and the front of his clothes were getting soaked. "I'm supposed to help Luke." He was close to tears.

"You're too little," Kelly said.

"Hey, hey!" Luke jumped up and pried the children apart. "None of that. Kelly, you pour the ice. Jacob, the salt."

Luke sat back down and Kelly, who was still wearing her long skirt, flounced dramatically over and poured more crushed ice from the bag into the bucket.

"Thatta girl. Now Jacob, how about more salt? Not too much, or the ice cream will freeze around the edges. There you go. Now what I need is some muscle."

Right on cue, Jacob put down the bag of salt, pushed up the sleeve of his white cotton shirt and flexed his muscle...or the place where a muscle should have been. With a great show of reverence, Luke felt the almost invisible bump. "Wow. You been lifting weights?"

Kelly giggled and looked over at her mother and Jenny. P.J. rolled her eyes skyward.

Luke pulled Jacob toward him. "Come around here in front of me."

Jacob came and stood so they were both facing the ice cream bucket. Luke put his hand over the boy's and together they began turning the old wooden handle.

"You can't crank too fast or the ice cream won't be smooth." Once Jacob got the hang of it, Luke took his hand away so the boy could do it by himself. "There you go," Luke said, encouragingly.

There was something about the sweet-mellow smell of a child that made Luke feel . . . well, homesick, was the word that came to mind. Only kids could smell that way, and he had always figured it was their innocence radiating from them.

Luke loved his godchildren. Kelly was all sunshine and open doors. Five-year-old Jacob was like the cool, soft moss that grew in the peaceful, shady places. Where Kelly was carefree and nothing seemed to bother her, Jacob took things to heart. Felt things more than other kids. There was a vulnerability about him that made Luke want to jump in and be his knight, do battle for him, protect him from the hurt that was dealt sensitive children by the outside world.

But one day last summer Luke had discovered that inside Jacob was a quiet strength that flowed like an underground spring waiting to be tapped.

When Jacob's pet rabbit had died of heat exhaustion, Luke had had to break the sad news to him. But he just couldn't seem to find the words. His throat had gotten tight and his eyes had stung. He'd had to turn away, pretending a sudden fascinated interest in the dry rot at the corner of the shed. He'd felt a shy tug on his pant leg and Jacob's voice had whispered up to him, "Don't be sad, Luke. I know you can't always make animals okay. Mom says only God can do that." There was a pause, then, "Maybe He wanted a nice rabbit for the kids in heaven to play with. Do you think so?"

Feeling as if his crusty bachelor's heart had been broken and put back together, all in the space of half a beat, Luke had turned and swung Jacob into his arms and together they had cried.

Old people and kids.

Luke looked down at the bucket and saw that the ice cream was thickening. Jacob reluctantly admitted that his arm was getting tired, so Kelly took her turn. Twenty cranks later, she'd had enough.

"It's Jenny's turn!" both children chorused.

Luke raised questioning eyebrows to Jenny.

"Go on." P.J. the matchmaker nudged her with an elbow.

"Okay." Jenny smiled and slid off the tailgate. She seemed almost as eager as Jacob and Kelly.

Luke pulled another lawn chair over next to him, wiggling it to make sure it was sitting level before she sat down.

Jenny wrapped her fingers around the wooden handle and began turning it, her expression serious and intent. From the uneven motion of the crank, Luke could tell the ice cream had gotten almost too thick for her.

"Here—" He put a hand over hers, helping to turn the paddle through the thickening cream. "Take it slow and steady."

Her head was next to his, and her soft hair tickled the side of his face. Under his rough palm, he could feel the delicate bones in her small hand. Remembering that she bruised easily, he was careful not to exert too much pressure.

It came to him again that he liked the way she smelled. He inhaled, pulling the sweet scent of her deep into his lungs. And through this bombardment of his senses a thought struck him and his hand stilled: he wanted her. He wanted Jenny May. Wanted to feel her soft breath against his skin, her soft lips on his.

Jenny turned her head so she could look at him. "Are we done?" she asked, her voice soft and a little husky, her eyes huge and dark, her lips full and moist and parted—and only inches away.

She was watching him, not moving. She was so close that he could feel her breath caress the side of his face. He could feel her hand under his, sense the rise and fall of her chest. If he leaned forward just a couple of inches, their lips would touch.

A yearning slammed through him, a yearning like he'd never known before. It staggered his senses, drove the air from his lungs.

"Is it done, is it done?" Jacob and Kelly chirped.

Like someone surfacing after a deep, deep dive, Luke groped his way back to his surroundings, to the fair, the children, the ice cream.

He let go of Jenny's hand and fell back in his chair, his heart knocking against his rib cage. With a shock, he realized that for a few seconds he'd completely lost track of where he was, who he was.

There had just been Jenny.

"No, the ice cream isn't done." P.J. was suddenly there, waving her arms, shooing the children away. "We have to put the strawberries in, then give it time to ripen."

"You two grown-ups run along and have your picnic, then come on back for ice cream."

So, the matchmaker was at it again, Luke thought wryly as he got to his feet.

P.J. viewed the world with idealistic naivety. Because of her own successful marriage, she just naturally thought everyone else's lives should follow the same pattern. She didn't see any reason why men and women shouldn't meet, get married, and live happily ever after.

A sense of deep melancholy hit him and for a few
seconds Luke found himself wishing that things could
be that easy, that innocent, that simple.

Chapter Seven

She'd fallen asleep on him. Luke had never had a date fall asleep on him before. It was always the other way around.

And so here he was, sitting on a slab of rock, watching the last glow of twilight turn to darkness while Jenny slept on a blanket behind him.

It was probably all for the best—gave his hormones time to cool, gave his head a chance to regain its proper perspective. He'd just been taken by surprise earlier, that's all. His hormones hadn't reacted that strongly in years. And that's all it was, he reminded himself again.

Hormones.

But apparently Jenny had the opposite problem. Her hormones had taken one look at his, yawned and fallen asleep. Not really an ego-building thing to have happen to a guy by any means.

An hour ago, Jenny had admitted to never having been on a picnic and hadn't seemed very enthused about it. It fact, he could have sworn she'd been dreading it. When he'd walked to his truck to get a blanket, he'd half expected her to bolt while he was away. But when he got back, he'd found her sitting in the shade at the edge of the creek, jeans rolled up, bare feet dangling in the clear water.

After that, things had gone pretty well. He'd even silently congratulated himself on his conduct. He hadn't teased her, hadn't asked her any personal questions. Shoot, he'd even kept a straight face when he'd opened the basket and seen those damned peanut butter sandwiches. No wonder she hadn't been very keen on the picnic.

And what had he gained by all that good behavior? She'd fallen asleep on him.

He locked the fingers of both hands together and stretched them over his head, knuckles popping.

Stella. He knew the picnic thing had been planned by Stella. It was just like her. But something had gone wrong. Boone had screwed it up somehow and Mason wound up with the ticket Luke should have drawn. It had taken him one look at his grandmother's surprised expression to figure the whole business out.

Normally, he would have just left it alone, let Jenny go with ol' Mace... but she'd been scared. And it was his fault. Obviously he'd played up the Bad Mason thing too much. Mason had done time in the pen, sure. For burning his draft card after seeing somebody on TV do it. Mason had never completely grown up. He was like a kid—still impressionable. But her panic had seemed out of proportion, and he wondered if there was more to it than simply fear of Mason....

Luke shook his head, then got to his feet. Well, he'd wake Sleeping Beauty and take her home.

Then he remembered that the Talbots were expecting them for ice cream. So he'd wake Jenny and they'd go have some ice cream, *then* he'd take her home.

He stopped at the edge of the blanket and looked down at her. The moon was coming up full and the night sky was clear, bathing everything in a milky, almost unreal light. Jenny was lying on her side, knees drawn partway to her chest, feet bare, head cradled on her inner arm, a strand of dark hair draped across one pale cheek.

He stood there a few seconds, then instead of waking her, he quietly stretched out beside her, elbow to the ground, head braced in his hand.

Lying there, he noticed little things about her. Like the way her dark lashes cast spiked shadows against her pale cheeks. He could see the delicate rise and fall of her chest, her breathing so soft that it was hard to tell if she breathed at all.

Fragile.

That was the word that popped into his head, the word for Jenny May. Everything about her whispered fragility and vulnerability. He suddenly had the over-whelming urge to pull her into his arms and protect her from something. But that was crazy. Protect her from what? It wasn't like him to let his imagination run away with him.

As he watched her, the feeling he'd had at the Tal-bots' camper started warming in him again, running through his veins like a low, steady hum.

He couldn't quit thinking about the way her soft lips had felt under his. What he wanted to do right now was kiss Jenny awake. Like in the fairy tale.

He leaned closer. Then he pressed his mouth to hers....

She responded, slowly at first. Her sleepy lips moved under his, as if they themselves were awaken-ing. And her lips were soft and sweet. God, but they were sweet. Then the rhythm of her breathing changed, and he knew she wasn't asleep anymore.

He pulled away just enough to look down at her, his hands braced against the blanket, on either side of her face.

Her brown eyes were as wide as a sleep-dazed child's. "Wh-what are you doing?" she whispered groggily up at him.

He smiled. "Peace talks. Engaging in peace talks."

She took some time thinking about that, and he re-alized she must still be disoriented from sleep. "Oh," she finally answered. Her huge, melting eyes shifted away from him, then back. He could see confusion in their depths.

"It's dark," she murmured. "I fell asleep."

"No kidding. Never had a date fall asleep on me before."

"I'm sorry." A frown creased her brow, as if she found the whole situation perplexing. "I usually never fall asleep."

He thought her statement a bit unusual, but chalked it up to disorientation. Everybody falls asleep.

She looked so warm and tousled, her eyes so huge and slumberous that he quickly forgot her peculiar comment. It might be peacetime, but inside Luke a battle was raging as he fought the urge to pull her into his arms and kiss her. *Really* kiss her.

The clean, fresh scent of her drifted up to him, making his head reel. And although he wasn't touching her, it seemed as if he was touching her. There was a space between them where the heat from their bodies collided, creating some kind of charged field.

That's when he gave up. Some things just weren't meant to be fought. He lowered himself beside her, wrapped his arms around her and pulled her close, the roundness of her breasts pressing against his chest.

Silently, she watched him, eyes wide, lips slightly parted. "What are you doing now?" She didn't sound frightened, only curious.

He reached up to stroke her hot cheek, then gently cradled her chin between his fingers and thumb. His gaze moved down her face to her full lips. "I'm going to kiss you." Then he remembered his promise to be polite. "Is that okay?"

"Yes." The word was whispered on a shallow breath.

"Good." He decided that there was definitely some merit to this polite stuff.

As soon as his lips touched hers she let out a small, contented sigh, a sigh that seemed to echo a response deep within his own chest. Fleetingly, he wondered if Jenny May might prove addictive.

He moved his mouth over hers with soft, tugging pulls. Her lips opened for him and he felt her hands sliding over his back, her fingers feathering across his ribs.

With the slight rationality he had left, he was once again astounded by the need he felt for her, the deep want. He released her chin. Beginning at her temple, he slid his fingers through her smooth hair to cup the back of her head. He could feel her heartbeat against his own, both doing double time.

He wanted her. Had to have her.

He dragged his mouth from hers, and she let out a small moan of protest and pulled him closer.

"Do you want this to happen?" he asked, a pulse beating in his head, his breath short and shallow.

"Yes." Her answer was almost as breathless. "I like it."

"Ah, Jenny." His head came down and her soft lips opened under his, urgently this time. A fire scorched through him. He shifted his weight and nudged a taut-muscled thigh between her legs. At first she stiffened, then relaxed. He moved his leg higher.

Jenny's world was spinning out of control, as if some stranger had invaded her thoughts, her body. Suddenly she craved and needed human contact, the contact she had always avoided, always denied herself before. But now she wanted to be touched by a man named Lucas Tate, wanted to feel him pull her close to his heart, feel the full weight of his body on hers.

"Jenny," he moaned against her mouth. "Sweet, sweet Jenny. I want you. Want to feel your skin against mine." With one hand, he tugged the hem of her shirt free of her jeans.

A gasp escaped her when she felt his rough palm make contact with the sensitive skin above her navel then skim her ribs.

"Lean this way." He pulled her closer so her weight was partially on him. With one hand, he reached behind her and unfastened her bra clasp.

A mild protest formed somewhere in the back of her mind, but it was quickly forgotten when he pressed her down to the ground and began kissing her again. All she was aware of was the heated feel of his hot, wet mouth on hers; the hardness of his thigh between her legs; his warm, rough hand on her bare breast, his thumb teasing the hardened nipple. She was a coiling, spiraling flame, whirling away into the night sky. . . .

Luke suddenly tore his lips from hers and buried his face into the hollow of her throat, his breath coming hard and fast. With her fingertips, she stroked his back, feeling his taut muscles through the soft cotton of his T-shirt. Gradually, the spiraling swirls behind her eyes calmed.

When he looked down at her, his lips were wet from their shared kisses, his eyes shining. A lock of hair had fallen over his forehead. And his hand still cupped her aching breast. "I'm acting like some high school kid," he rasped out. Slowly, he pulled his hand free of her shirt, then sat up, bringing her with him.

All she could do was watch in a heat-flushed daze as he reached under her shirt with both hands, adjusted her bra, fastened it, then let her shirt fall back down.

Little by little, she became aware of her surroundings: the damp feel of the ground through the coarse blanket; the scent of dew-laden grass; the chirping of crickets and the deep croak of bullfrogs. A murmur of far-off voices and faint carnival music carried to them on the night air.

Luke kissed her on the mouth quick and hard, then got to his feet. "Come on. Let's go to my house." He held out a hand for her to grab. "I don't think you want to make love with the fairgrounds so close."

Jenny's breath caught in her throat and her mind reeled. *Make love?* He thought she wanted to make love?

Of course he did, a voice in her head mocked. Why wouldn't he? She hadn't protested in the least. In fact, in five more minutes, she most likely would have been helping *him* undress.

Heat flooded her face, and she was thankful for the semidarkness. She turned away and began putting on her shoes and socks, giving the chore her undivided attention. When she was done, she took a deep breath, then blurted out, "I'm not coming to your house."

"What?" The picnic basket lid slammed, making her jump.

Not looking at him, she got to her feet, then picked up the blanket, fighting the panic that was setting in. "I'm not coming to your house. It's after eight." She gave the blanket a good shake, aware that he was moving toward her.

"What the hell does that have to do with anything?"

Jenny hadn't had much experience in dealing with men. At the all-girls school she'd attended, there hadn't been much opportunity to meet boys. A lot of girls had sneaked out after lockup, but Jenny never had. That left the chaperoned dances and stiff formal dinners where they could exchange witty conversation with nervous boys from a neighboring boys' school. To Jenny, such evenings had been nothing but uncomfortable fiascoes to somehow muddle through as best she could, then forget.

When she'd gotten older, she'd never dated anyone seriously. She didn't know why, really. Maybe because to date someone seriously, to have a *relationship*, you had to open up to them, reveal things about yourself. In other words, make yourself vulnerable and she could never do that.

Of course there had been Jeffrey—a friend in her relief unit. They had gone to a few movies together and afterward he'd always left her at the doorstep with a dry, tight-lipped kiss.

And that was the extent of her experience in dealing with the opposite sex. She knew most people would probably consider it odd by today's standards. Twenty-four and never been with a man....

"I said, what does eight o'clock have to do with anything?"

Words tumbled from her. "I—I only had to stay with you till eight o'clock."

In the heavy silence that followed, she could feel his anger building.

"*Had* to?" he finally roared in disbelief. "You're talking like somebody twisted your arm. Listen, you never *had* to be with me at all. I was doing you a favor when I traded tickets!"

His body was a rigid silhouette against the dim light coming from the fairgrounds, and Jenny was thankful that the moon was at her back so he couldn't see her face. She took a deep, shaky breath, praying that he wouldn't be able to tell from her voice that she was very close to tears. "You shouldn't have kissed me." She clutched the scratchy blanket to her chest, as if it could protect her, as if it somehow made a shield between herself and Luke.

"Oh, yeah?" He took a step closer and jerked the blanket from her hands, balling it up and jamming it under his arm. "Pardon me, but if memory serves me right, I *asked*, and you told me you were willing. As I understood it, you were more than willing. You as much as said you *wanted* me."

It was true. She did—*had* wanted him, she frantically corrected.

But he had overwhelmed her. When he'd touched her and kissed her, it was as if she'd been engulfed by a tidal wave. The sand had been sucked from under her feet, knocking her down and dragging her into its fierce undertow. She'd been helpless. And the thought of someone having that kind of power over her was frightening.

She'd let her guard down. She'd opened the door and let Luke in. Now she had to close the door, protect herself.

She pulled on her invisible cloak and drew herself up straighter. Tilting her head back, she looked up at him. "I won't be staying at your grandmother's much longer."

He was watching her with the moonlight reflected in his eyes, making them glow like some wild animal's. Her show of false bravado faltered and she drew in a trembling breath. "Until I go, will you please leave me alone?" She had to turn her back quickly and press her fingers to her mouth to stop her lips from trembling, stop the sob rising in her.

Behind her, Jenny could feel his silence. Then she heard him sigh. "Jenny—don't leave because of me." All trace of anger was gone. His voice was low, thoughtful. "Come on. I'll take you home, then I won't bother you anymore. I promise."

Her throat was thick with tears and all she could manage was a quick shake of her head.

"Jenny—" A pause. "I'm sorry."

"Go! Just go!" Her breath caught. She held the air deep in her lungs, welcoming the distraction of physical discomfort, listening. . . .

Then she finally heard what she was waiting for, or what she tried to convince herself she was waiting for: the sound of Luke moving away through the grass, leaving behind the cricket calls, the occasional croak of a bullfrog.

Night sounds. Lonely sounds.

Before Luke left the fairgrounds, he found Stella and let her know that Jenny would be needing a ride home. After that, he made some lame excuse to the Talbots, which he was sure didn't fool P.J. for a minute. Then he took off down the backroads, engine roaring, windows cranked down, a hot night wind tugging at his hair, the dew-covered cornfields he passed smelling green and damp. From the dashboard, the AM radio glowed orange, spewing out a static-filled pesticide commercial, occasionally punctuated by backfire from the truck's split tailpipe.

He reached out and flicked off the radio.

What the hell had happened back there?

He'd scared her. And he'd made her cry.

He'd hurt her. In some way he didn't understand, he'd hurt her. A painful, self-mocking laugh tore from him. Here he was, the guy who was supposed to stop pain, not cause it.

In his mind, he searched back over the last hour, trying to figure it out, make some sense of it. One minute, he'd been flying, thinking she was flying right along with him, then *pow*, she'd done a hundred-and-eighty-degree turn. At the time, he hadn't recognized it for what it was, but now he could see that he must have come on too strong and she'd panicked.

I don't think you want to make love with the fairgrounds so close.

That was it. The trigger. He'd suggested they go to his house, then there had been instant panic. Virginal panic? Considering the mobile life she'd led, it just didn't seem likely.

His thoughts drifted back to the first time he'd kissed her. Her hair had been tied back and she been wearing that big white shirt. He wasn't the kind of guy who grabbed women and kissed them, but that day he couldn't have stopped himself if he'd tried.

And when he'd pulled away, her cheeks had been bright red. She'd been flustered, embarrassed. At the time he thought it might have been because of the circumstances, but now he didn't know.... Now he was beginning to wonder if maybe Jenny wasn't accustomed to being touched, being kissed.

Then he thought about all the times she'd drawn away, all the times she'd put up an invisible wall, as if she had some deep hurt that she didn't want anybody to see, didn't want anybody to suspect.

More than anything, he wanted to help her. But how could he when it seemed that he was one of her problems, possibly the direct cause of her unhappiness? That would be like the Big Bad Wolf offering to help Little Red Riding Hood.

If the problem *was* him, if his presence distressed her so much, he would just have to make sure their paths didn't cross.

It certainly wasn't a solution that satisfied him, and the melancholy feeling he'd had earlier settled in his chest again. Before going home, he swung by Ellison General Store and picked up a pack of cigarettes.

Chapter Eight

Carrying a bowl of milk, Jenny slipped out the screen door, the gray enamel of the porch cool under her bare feet. Putting down the bowl near the bottom step, she called to Max, and the kitten appeared from around the corner, furtively creeping up to the milk.

In her childhood, Jenny hadn't had a pet to care for, and it made her feel good to see the once scrawny animal looking so much healthier.

She settled herself into the wicker rocker, pressing her toes against the floor, starting the chair to rocking gently. Her eyes were drawn across the road to where an endless sea of green corn met a motionless sky. Occasionally, she could hear what sounded like the deep rumble of far-off thunder. No breeze so much as stirred a single blade of the tall, heat-curled stalks.

She'd had no idea that corn grew so tall. If she were to stand among them, the stalks would tower over her.

The evening air was close, heavy, a little smothering, and the sky, beneath thick clouds, had a strange yellow cast. There was much talk about the heat and the need for moisture. A few days ago some pattering sprinkles had fallen, but everyone's hopes for a good soaking rain had been short-lived. It hadn't been enough of a shower to settle the dust.

And through it all, through all the hot, dry days and long, lonely nights, Lucas Tate had kept his promise.

Three weeks had gone by since the day of the fair. Twice Jenny had run into Luke at Stella's. On both occasions he'd immediately made an excuse and left. Other than that, Jenny hadn't seen him except for the times he'd roared past her house in his beat-up truck, three dogs of mixed sizes and breeds in back, their noses pointed into the wind, music and dust billowing behind.

Two of those times Jenny had been in the front yard, but Luke hadn't glanced in her direction. And both times a sense of loss had washed over her and a small twist of pain had lodged somewhere below her heart.

She had asked that he leave her alone, and he had.... But what else could she have done?

Then there had been the bicycle. Someone had left it leaning under the oak tree in the front yard. Jenny assumed it had been Danny Talbot, but when she rode to the gas station in order to pay and thank him, he told her he'd never worked on it.

In fact, Danny had taken one look at the bike and told her he hadn't laid eyes on it for at least fifteen years. Then he began reminiscing about the old days, telling her that it didn't seem all that long ago that Luke had chopped several winters' worth of wood to save up for that bike.

Luke. The bike belonged to Luke, and he'd never even mentioned it.

A slow, wistful smile tugged at the corners of Jenny's mouth as she thought about Luke with Newt's cats, Luke with Jacob and Kelly. Luke with her....

What else could she have done?

There had been a few times—times too brief to fully grasp—when she'd felt a thawing within herself, when it seemed as if her frozen veins had been touched by rays of warm sunshine—radiant, magical.

Remembering, Jenny brought up her hand, touching her bottom lip with one finger.

He'd kissed her awake....

When Luke had touched her, pulled her close, her head had spun and she'd lost all sense of self, lost her equilibrium. She'd been hypnotized, mesmerized. At that moment she would have gone anywhere with him, done anything. And that scared her. She couldn't allow herself to be around someone who confused her the way Luke did, who caused her to feel and do things totally foreign to her nature.

But ever since that day of the picnic she'd often found herself wondering what it would have been like if she'd taken his hand and gone with him.

But she hadn't.

She knew her emotions were lying close to the surface. Again and again she'd told herself that under other circumstances—if she'd met Luke six weeks ago, before Mexico—she would have been able to deal with him. But right now she was vulnerable. What few defenses she had left were brittle and eggshell thin.

Sleep.

She needed sleep, craved sleep, longed for sleep, for the normal kind, the kind she'd taken for granted before Mexico. The dreamless kind of sleep she'd had the day of the fair, when Luke had been beside her.

Even though the thermometer of the old barn hadn't dropped below seventy in weeks, Jenny was cold inside, in her bones. Sometimes she thought she was cold all the way to her soul. And the dreams still came. No matter how she scolded herself, no matter how much she told herself that it was childish to be frightened of the dark, of dreams, it didn't help. And not only had the dreams persisted, they'd become worse, building, feeding on one another until sleep, the restful kind, was only a shadowy memory from some other life.

Sometimes her hands would shake, and she'd find herself watching them with detachment, as if she were on the outside of everything, even herself. Part of the remoteness was due to exhaustion. At times, she was fatigued to the point of light-headedness. And still sleep eluded her.

Last week she'd purposely tried to wear herself out. She had worked in the yard, weeding and hoeing—but not too zealously. She didn't want to force the flowers and shrubs to remain within established boundaries, she only wanted to keep them from being choked out.

After finishing with the yard she had moved on to the house, spending two days painting the trim. And every night she'd fallen into bed exhausted, but not too exhausted to dream.

Never too exhausted to dream.

For Jenny, it seemed that everything had changed, yet nothing had changed. Sometimes the very peace of the country contrasted so starkly with her inner torment that it seemed to mock her, dangling before her its unachievable tranquility: a state of mind she feared she'd never experience again.

She had come here looking for something, on a sort of spiritual quest, hoping the quiet and solitude of the country would soothe her shattered nerves. The healing she'd sought had evaded her, but something else had happened, something totally unexpected.

Ellison, Iowa had taken hold of her, enchanted her. At times she felt as if she'd stepped right into the cream-colored pages of Thornton Wilder's *Our Town*.

She'd had visitors—callers, as Newt had so quaintly put it when he'd come to ask about the kitten's welfare. He'd even invited Jenny to his house to play a few games of gin rummy. And P.J. Talbot had come by, with her kids in tow—Kelly and sweet little Jacob.

Callers . . .

But there comes a time to reach the end of the book, let go of the people inside and close the cover. She couldn't stay here forever, couldn't hide here forever. She had to leave, pick up the threads of her old life, and, she hoped, get in with her old relief unit.

A thought came to her, a thought she tried to push aside, tried to ignore, but couldn't: when she returned to work, would she be able to handle it anymore?

She would make herself. She had to. That was all there was to it.

While she'd been sitting, the orange glow in the sky had turned to gray, bringing with it dusk and a familiar dread. Jenny hated this time of day, didn't want to think about facing all the hours that loomed so endlessly ahead of her. Until now, she'd never known nights could be so long, so dark, so lonely.

Again she wondered what would have happened, what her life would be like right now if she'd taken Luke's hand.

The presence. It was with Jenny again. Close. Very close.

She fought it. Tried to come up for air, tried to tear herself free of its tenacious grip, but she couldn't move. Her joints were paralyzed. Heaviness pressed down on her chest, trapping her. A scream formed on her lips but died before it could be turned to sound, remaining only a terrified echo in her mind.

The dream. Always the dream.

She recognized the pattern. By now it was very familiar. Always the same. Always intensifying. Like the frantic strains of an orchestra gone wild, crescendoing to an ear-shattering finale when the cymbals crash together and the invisible presence is set free.

Building. Always building....

Wake up. Wake up.

In her sleep, she grappled and clawed with her nightmare, trying to escape its suffocating embrace, trying to run, to move. And all the while, the presence was there, behind her, pulsing closer. Always closer. Jenny could feel its hot breath stirring against the back of her neck, its power smothering her, pulling her down under the murky surface of a bottomless lake.

The cymbals crashed.

Jenny gasped and came awake with a start, sitting bolt upright. Her throat hurt, burned with every breath she took. She shivered. Her gown was sweat-soaked, her hair clinging to her face and neck in damp tendrils.

Outside, rain beat at the windows, propelled by gusts of wind. Thunder rumbled in the distance.

The disorientation left by the dream began to fade, and with a cold chill she realized the room was engulfed in darkness.

Black as a tomb.

Oh, God. The light—what had happened to the light? Was she even awake? Or was this part of the dream? Was she still caught up in the web of her nightmare?

Like a blind person, she lifted one hand to feel her face. Her eyes were open wide. A trembling breath escaped her parted lips. She brought her hand back down, feeling the softness of the bed beneath her, the damp tangle of sheets around her bare legs.

The storm had caused the power to go off.

No.

Her mind refused the obvious. She pressed her eyes shut, stomach sick with fear. That was too unthinkable—to be without electricity, to be without light. The light bulb had burned out. That's all. The light bulb.

She sat there in the dark, fingers pressing the sheet to her rapidly beating heart, listening to her ragged breathing, listening to the windowpanes rattle, feeling that the very walls shuddered around her.

She would get up, walk across the room, and turn on the overhead light. Easy. Push the little black button and the darkness would be chased away.

She tugged the twisted sheet from her legs, wishing that she was wearing more than the flimsy nightgown. Sometimes she slept fully clothed—she felt less vulnerable that way. But tonight she'd forced herself to be reasonable, to quit being so childish.

She swung her feet to the floor, sat there for a minute gathering her nerve, then stood up. She drew a deep, shaky breath, then moved across the room, arms extended in front of her like a sleepwalker. When she came to the wall, she groped along. Something shifted under her fingers.

Crash.

It seemed that her heart stopped, then started again.

A picture. She'd knocked down the picture of a cottage that hung near the door. And the switch was to the right of where the picture had been. When her fingers came in contact with the smooth rectangular plate, she let out her breath in relief and pushed the button.

Click.

Nothing happened. Oh, God. What she had refused to believe was true. The power was out.

A fresh wave of panic washed over her and she felt her flesh creep in renewed terror. What was she going to do now? Stay where she was? Try to make it back to the bed?

The rain continued to beat its deafening tattoo on the outer walls, the roof, the windows. Beneath all the noise there was a hollow roaring in Jenny's head, as if conch shells were being held to her ears.

Be strong, she told herself sternly. She wasn't a child, afraid to look in the closet, afraid of what lurked under the bed. She was an adult, must act like an adult.

It was only a storm. A power line had been knocked down or something, that was all. There was nothing in this room to be afraid of, nothing in this house to fear.

All she had to do was go downstairs to the kitchen and get the matches from the drawer by the back door.

In her mind's eye, she could see the oil lamps that someone had left on the top shelf in the cellar. All Jenny had to do was get to them.

Easy. Simple. Child's play. Like a game of blindman's buff.

She could hear her own ragged breathing coming from deep inside her, the sound filling the room. Outside, the rain beat down.

Adrenaline was charging through her veins. Her thoughts had gone into overdrive, rushing ahead, tripping over each other.

She couldn't take the darkness, had to get rid of the darkness. That was the important thing. First things first. Finish one chore before starting another. Start with number one. Begin at the beginning. A walk of a thousand miles begins with a single step. . . .

Who had said that? Confucius? Einstein? Neil Armstrong? No, that was one small step for man—

Hand gripping the doorjamb, she shushed her rambling thoughts and focused all of her attention on moving from the room. On moving—period. She slid a bare foot forward, the floorboard creaking under her light weight. Instead of being smooth and cool, the wood was tacky from the sudden increase in humidity.

Her eyes were open so wide they hurt, but she still couldn't see any variance in the blackness before her. There wasn't a hint of a shape, not a rectangle of gray that might suggest a window. The sensation was like walking into and through a penetrable wall.

Here in the country there was no glow from street-lights to seep in around curtains, no headlight beams to handily illuminate an occasional path so a person could find her way to the bathroom or refrigerator. Here it was black upon black.

People who live in towns have no idea what darkness, real darkness is, Jenny decided. They go along thinking that their shadowy world with its vague shapes is called dark, but it's not.

The second Jenny's fingers made contact with the cool wood of the banister, she felt a little better. She knew where she was, knew if she kept a grip on the railing, it would lead her downstairs. It was the wide-open places that were hard to navigate.

She took it slowly, knowing she had reached the bottom when her foot touched the braided rug that lay on the floor in front of the last step.

She stopped, then turned left and let go of the handrail. She was concentrating so hard on using senses usually taken for granted that her fear was receding into the background and the confusion that always followed her dream was fading.

She was carefully inching her way to the kitchen when her toe connected with a chair leg.

"Damn!" Her pain-filled voice rang out in the still, humid air.

She lifted her foot to rub her toe. Then she tried her voice again, finding she liked hearing it.

"Damn." Cussing made her feel braver. A small defiance against the darkness.

She began moving again and made it to the kitchen. Six more steps took her to the counter. She found the drawer, pulled it open, and quickly ran her fingers across the objects inside, trying to determine what was what. It made her think of the child's game where the players reach into a paper bag and guess the contents.

She touched a clothespin—the straight kind, without the spring—the kind that can be used for making wooden soldiers. She'd been hanging up her laundry outside, liking the way it smelled when she brought it in to fold it.

Loose change... A penny. She felt a penny. Or was it a nickle? Blind people wanted the nickle to be made eight-sided so it could be distinguished from a penny. That seemed like a good idea.

She continued to grope. Coupons, pencils, a tablet, paper clips... Where were the matches?

The tip of her fingers scraped across a small, abrasive-edged piece of thin cardboard.

A matchbook.

She grabbed it, untucking the cover to make sure there were plenty of matches inside. Almost full. She let out a breath.

Okay. She'd gotten from point A to point B. Now all she had to do was get from point B to C. In another few minutes she'd be home free.

With shaky fingers she tore a match loose and struck it. After such total darkness, the single tiny flame seemed to light the whole room, casting eerie, bobbing shadows against the walls and ceiling.

She moved forward, in the direction of the green cellar door, cupping the flame in her hands as she went. When the heat touched her fingers, she shook out the match and lit another.

By the third match, she was half way down the cellar steps.

The cellar was one of Jenny's least favorite places. It had a dirt floor, a musty smell and rough stone walls with recesses that made her think of catacombs. But she could do it. She'd made it this far, hadn't she? Child's play.

From above and behind her, the phone shrilled.

Jenny jerked, the match went out, and she missed the step. Her hand flailed for the two-by-four railing she knew was there, but only met with clammy air. Then she was pitching forward, and with one of those strange, fleeting moments of chilling insight that come with sudden accidents, she knew she wouldn't be able to catch herself, knew she must fall, knew that after all it wasn't child's play because children shouldn't play with matches.

The next thing she was aware of was lying on her side on the packed clay floor, the uneven stone wall at her back, body aching, her head full of cellar smells— smells of damp ground and musty stonework. She had no idea how long she'd been there, she only knew the phone was no longer ringing.

With Jenny, smells had always had a way of conjuring up memories. Her scent-evoked images were so vivid that at times it was like being there, like having her own built-in time machine.

A single whiff of the one hundred dollar an ounce fragrance her mother had always used, and Jenny would find herself a child again, hiding behind a white velvet loveseat, listening to party chatter and watching evening gowns glide past.

It was the same with Play-Doh. Whenever she smelled it, the years simply fell away and she was transported back to a time before boarding schools and finishing schools, to when she used to go to her neighbor, Cindy Keller's, and create all sorts of wonderful things.

But olfactory glands weren't choosy. It made no difference to them whether the images they evoked were good or bad, whether they brought a feeling of nostalgic happiness...or struck terror to a person's soul.

It was the same now.

The last several weeks simply crumbled away as if they had never been. Jenny was in Mexico again, trapped within the cold earth, beneath tons of concrete and steel.

Buried alive.

It hadn't been Jenny's job to go inside the earthquake-riddled buildings. As driver of the relief truck, it was her duty to make sure the vehicle arrived at the disaster area well stocked. On that particular day, she had made it to the site before the rest of the crew and had immediately begun unloading supplies and setting up the emergency station.

As she unpacked, she became aware of a faint, metallic tapping sound, so repetitive that it was noticeable even with the distant wailing of the sirens.

Tap, tap, tap.

The sound came from one of the collapsed buildings.

Never asking herself whether she should or shouldn't go, she grabbed a survival pack and flashlight from the truck and hurried in the direction of the distress signal. Along one side of the crumbled building was a long fissure, just wide enough for Jenny to squeeze through. Slowly, she moved toward the sound, eventually having to get down and crawl with the flashlight in one hand.

Ten minutes later, deep within the rubble, she found a trapped, injured man. Immobilized by a slab of cement, he was using a metal pocketknife to tap against a pipe, the sound following the cylinder to the outside.

Jenny talked to him, telling him that help would be along—to hang on and everything would be okay. He thanked her, his voice tight and filled with pain. In the cramped, dark pit it was impossible to determine how severely he was injured. All she could do was reassure him, tell him that she was going for help.

She had barely begun to inch her way back through the shaft of cement when a low rumble started, and the ground under her hands began to shift and tremble.

Aftershocks.

She felt herself slipping, heard a scream and wondered if it came from her. Then everything went black.

When she came to, she was lying facedown, her lungs raw from breathing chalky dust. There was a crushing pressure on her shoulder and back. And she couldn't see anything.

At first, she thought she might be dead. But if that were the case, then surely her shoulder wouldn't hurt so much, surely her lungs wouldn't ache with raw pain every time she took a breath....

How long would it take to die here? How long would the air hold out?

She spent what must have been several hours drifting in and out of semiconsciousness. In one of her more lucid moments she remembered the injured man and her confident promise to bring help.

"Mr...Mr—" she managed to rasp, her hoarse voice echoing eerily around her. "Are you okay?"

No answer. Not a whisper, not a scuttle of soil, not a breath... Not a tap...

Then she remembered the flashlight and survival pack. They had to be nearby.

She tried to move, but her body was trapped, wedged between tons of concrete and steel. The only thing she could move was her left arm.

Slowly, she felt around her, hoping against hope that she would touch the flashlight and that it would still work.

Stretching . . . groping . . . feeling. . . .

Her fingertips brushed against something unfamiliar, something that wasn't cement, wasn't crumbling dirt.

She jerked her hand away, heart thundering, thundering, head spinning, recoiling in denial.

It couldn't be. It just couldn't be.

After what seemed like eons, she forced her frozen fingers to move, to return to the place they'd been before. To stretch, to feel, to prove to herself that she'd been mistaken . . .

Then she touched it.

Flesh. Cold, clammy flesh.

Oh, God, no!

She screamed and screamed until her voice gave out, until blessed unconsciousness took her again.

Time passed, possibly days passed, and her thoughts became more incoherent and confused. Reality mixed with unreality.

Once, when she was little, she'd seen a show on TV—maybe *The Twilight Zone* or *Outer Limits*—she wasn't sure, but she'd never been able to forget it.

The story had been about a man serving a life sentence. He wanted to escape and knew the only way to get out of prison was by dying. As luck would have it, a prisoner did just that. After arranging for the nutty prison doctor to dig him up later that night, the man hid inside the coffin with the covered corpse. The coffin was nailed shut, carried outside and buried in the cemetery. The escapee waited and waited for the old man, his oxygen dwindling, his nerves becoming as thin and taut as piano wire.

But the doctor never came.

In the last frame of the show, the escapee lit a match to look at his watch. The sheet fell away from behind him, revealing not the dead prisoner, but the dead doctor, the only person who knew of the plan.

Jenny had had nightmares about that show for a long, long time. Years. And now reality and fiction seemed to have intertwined, making her heart race in terror, her breath come short and fast. And like the prisoner in the coffin, she couldn't face the horrible **realization** that she would die here, and that her last hours would be shared with a corpse.

Tears stung her eyes, trailing down her cheeks, mixing with the dirt.

No one was coming for her.

Hush little baby, don't you cry.

Three days.

It took the rescue workers three days to find her. She and the dead man were carried out together.

From upstairs came a pounding, bringing Jenny back to a fuzzy reality, still caught up in the horrors of her nightmare. She was only vaguely aware of the cold earth under her cheek, the cold, sweating stones at her back. Like a grave.

Then even that began to fade....

The pounding came again, more urgently this time.

"Jenny!"

Luke's voice. A voice she would recognize in the darkest dark.

"Jenny!"

She should answer him, tell him where she was. That's what she should do, but she was so tired....

A door creaked. Then footsteps sounded against hardwood...fading, moving upstairs, to the bedrooms. Back and forth, in a hurry. Doors opening, doors closing. Then the footsteps moved back down the stairs to the first floor.

"Jenny!" Boot soles ringing against linoleum tile.

"Jenny!"

With supreme effort, Jenny forced her eyes open, then somehow managed to push herself to her knees.

A tiny rectangle of light could be seen at the top of the cellar steps, where she'd left the door ajar.

Slow footsteps moved closer. They stopped at the top of the stairs. The cellar door creaked all the way open and she was blinded by a beam of light. She put up a protective arm and turned her face to the wall, away from the brightness. The light shifted from her face.

"Jenny."

She knew the person at the top of the stairs was Luke, but his normally distinguishable voice was almost unrecognizable. He sounded so odd.

As if it hurt for him to talk.

Chapter Nine

Luke stood at the top of the stairs, trying to pull himself together.

When he'd turned the flashlight into the cellar and seen Jenny, seen the smear of blood on her forehead, seen her dirt-smudged face with tracks left by her tears, he'd felt himself falling apart. Immediately, he'd beamed the light away—it had seemed such an intrusion, an invasion. Now he wanted to bolt down the steps and convince himself that she was okay.

But she wasn't okay.

One look at her told him she wasn't okay. He could sense the fragile hold she had on herself, sense that she was fighting for control. So he told himself to take it slow, take it easy. The last thing he wanted to do was upset her any more than she already was.

"Jenny."

He spoke her name quietly, soothingly, trying to reach out to her with his voice, the single word seeming to hang within the damp walls of the cellar.

Still on her knees, Jenny raised one hand, distractedly attempting to push her tangled hair back from her face, only to have it fall forward again. And still she smoothed it, over and over. She wouldn't look in his direction, but kept her eyes focused straight ahead, toward the dark recesses of the cellar.

"I—I fell down the last steps." Her voice came out as a high quaver, edged with hysteria. "But I'm okay. I don't need any help."

Having no idea how badly she was hurt, he set the flashlight on the landing, directing the beam along the wood-plank ceiling. Then he started down the steps, forcing himself to take them slowly, one at a time.

"Don't come down here!"

The desperation in her voice bounced off the stone walls and echoed up the steps toward him.

He forced himself to stop, fighting the overwhelming urge to get her up the stairs, get her out of the damp, dark cellar as quickly as possible. "Jenny, I can't leave you here like this."

She locked her arms at her waist, hugging herself. "I don't need your help." Her voice was a thin thread of sound, winding higher. "I'm not hurt."

He took another step, the old wood creaking and giving under his weight. "Your head's bleeding. Let me look at it."

With one hand, she touched her temple, then drew her hand away, looking at the blood on her fingers as if surprised to find it there. "I—I'm okay." Shakily, she got to her feet and faced him, arms at her sides.

Her eyes, when she finally looked directly at him, were anxious, a little wild. "See?" She made a stiff gesture with both arms. "I'm all right."

Nothing could have been further from the truth.

Even in the dingy light, Luke could see the smudges on her cheeks, see the smear of blood across her forehead. Her white knee-length gown was dirty. So were her arms, her legs. She'd been lying there hurt and alone on the dirt floor, in the dark....

He swallowed, his throat feeling tight.

Again, she pushed a tangle of hair back, and as she did he saw that her hand shook. "I—I came down to get a lamp..."

Jenny, Jenny.

It hurt him to see her like this, and he had to fight to keep his own voice steady. "Come upstairs with me and I'll come back for the lamp. Then I'll leave." He had no intention of leaving, but he would deal with that once he got her upstairs.

She gave a slow, defeated nod, hands hanging limply at her sides. Her dark eyes, when she looked up at him, had lost some of their wildness. Now they were glazed pools, filled with a resigned exhaustion.

What was going on here? What had happened to put such a lost look in those sad eyes? If he didn't know better, he'd say she was suffering from some kind of emotional shock.

She swayed, and his hands lashed out to steady her. Her skin was clammy and cold like the cellar, and he wondered how long she had been down here.

"I'm okay," she protested feebly, not sounding okay at all. Not sounding okay in the least. She tried to pull away, but he wouldn't let her.

Jenny, Jenny.

More than anything, he wanted to pull her close, comfort her, at least pick her up in his arms and carry her upstairs. But he was afraid of scaring her. So instead he secured his arm around her, steadying her against him and led her up the steps.

Close, but not too close.

When they reached the kitchen, he dragged out a chair and pushed her down on it, then went back to retrieve the flashlight. He balanced it on the table, lens up, so the beam reflected off the white ceiling, casting enough light for him to see inside the kitchen drawers. He searched through them until he found a small towel, then went to the sink and twisted the cold water tap. There was enough air pressure left in the tank for one last blast of water, enough to wet the towel.

When he turned around, Jenny was sitting with her chin to her chest, eyes closed.

"Jenny."

Gently, he grasped her by the chin, tilting her head up so he could see the cut better.

Her eyelids came open and she regarded him with huge, haunted eyes. "I don't like the dark, you know," she told him with all the solemnity of a child.

Her quiet confession broke his heart and sent a chill through him at the same time.

Jenny, Jenny.

What are you hiding from? What are you running from? What terrible thing has happened to you? What terrible thing has made you afraid of the dark? He wanted to ask, but knew this wasn't the time.

He lifted the cloth. "This will hurt a little."

"That's okay."

With careful strokes, he cleaned the dried blood and dirt from around the edges of the cut near her hairline. While he worked, she continued to watch him, her expression never altering, eyes never straying from his face.

"Stitches?" she asked so faintly he almost didn't hear her.

He frowned and slanted her forehead toward the light, feeling around the cut itself for signs of a deeper injury. He couldn't find any. The cut was no more than a deep scratch. "Butterfly bandage should do the trick. I've got some out in the truck. Wait here and I'll be right back."

He hurried to the truck and returned carrying a small first aid kit. Jenny was sitting exactly as he'd left her, quietly staring ahead. Now there was an artificial calm about her that worried him as much as her earlier panic.

When he cleaned her forehead with disinfectant, she never flinched. Then he placed a butterfly bandage over the cut, pulling the skin together as he smoothed the sides down. "Shouldn't even have a scar," he told her when he'd finished.

Her eyelids fluttered closed, and for an alarmed second he thought maybe she was going to faint.

"Thanks," she whispered in an utterly exhausted voice.

He wondered if she'd hit her head when she'd fallen down the steps. She had some of the symptoms of a concussion—slurred speech, sleepiness.

He picked up the flashlight and checked her pupils. They responded to the light. He felt her head for a bump or contusion, but couldn't find anything. She seemed to be wiped out, drained of all energy, like a marathon runner who had been pushed beyond her limit of endurance.

He picked up the towel and gently stroked the smudges from her cheeks until her face was clean. Then he washed her arms, one at a time.

Her legs—they were dirty, too. Especially her knees.

He tried not to think of the familiarity of what he was about to do, tried to forget that she was half-dressed, reminding himself to keep some distance. After all, he was a doctor, wasn't he? He knew all about medical distance. And even though most of his patients were animals, there had been several times when he'd been called upon to treat people during emergencies.

He crouched down in front of her and settled her foot against his jean-clad thigh. She had such small, perfect feet. . . .

"Mmm. That feels good," she mumbled in a thick voice as he finished one leg, then moved to the other. When he was done, she let out a sigh and he looked up. She was about ready to slide right out of the chair.

"Better get you up to bed."

He handed her the flashlight. "Hang on to this." Never hesitating this time, he swung her into his arms. She hardly seemed heavier than Jacob.

One of her arms flopped in the air. "To bed, to bed." Her voice was slurred by exhaustion.

Once upstairs, he put her down on the edge of the bed, but she immediately fell across it on her back, flashlight rolling from her hand to the mattress, its beam directed toward the door.

What was he supposed to do now? Her gown was wet and filthy. He could hardly let her crawl into bed like that.

Distance, he reminded himself. Distance.

He snatched up the flashlight, strode to the dresser and began opening and shutting drawers. When he couldn't find anything that looked even remotely like a nightgown, he pulled out a white T-shirt and held it up. It was big, and it was long. It ought to do.

He strode back to the bed. "Up you go." He pulled her back to a sitting position. Her head lolled forward, eyes closed. "Sleep," she mumbled. "Let me sleep."

"Sorry I have such a peculiar effect on you. Just hang on a little longer, then you can sleep for the next two days if you want."

He thought he detected a flicker of a smile at that.

"You can't crawl into bed wearing those dirty clothes," he told her—although he could remember doing precisely that on more than one occasion. But women were different. They didn't do stuff like that.

Her eyelids lifted just a fraction and she looked down at herself. "Oh," was her sage comment. With limp arms, she reached up, stripped the offending gown from her body and slapped it to the floor. "There." She rolled away, her back to him, bikini panties the only article of clothing left on her.

What had he done to deserve this? He was trying to be a gentleman, but she wasn't making it easy.

With a stoic sigh, he sat down on the edge of the bed, the mattress dipping with his weight. "Jenny. Come on. You've got to put this on." He managed to pull her back to a sitting position, leaning her against his chest so he could use both hands to grapple with the T-shirt he was holding behind her.

"You smell good," she mumbled against his throat, her breath a caress.

He had the neck hole of the shirt ready when she suddenly flung her arms around him, pressing herself to his chest. "Rain. You smell like rain."

It wasn't until then that he realized his shirt was wet from the storm. "Jenny—" With one hand, he tried to pry her away, but she clung tightly, snuggling closer.

Good Lord.

He gave up trying to put the shirt on her. He was no masochist. Anyway, the room wasn't cold. Hell, no. Now that the rain had stopped the air was humid and a little steamy. And getting steamier all the time.

With both hands, he reached up and forcefully unlocked her fingers from the back of his neck. "Lie down and go to sleep." He pushed her gently back on the bed, then pulled the sheet up around her shoulders. She burrowed deeper, drawing her knees up, her hair lying in dark contrast against the white of the embroidery-edged pillow case.

He took off his wet shirt and hung it on the bedpost, flicked off the flashlight and lay down on his back beside her, careful to stay on top of the covers, careful not to touch her.

Then, tucking his hands behind his head, he stared up at the empty blackness above him, wondering what he was going to do about Jenny.

He thought she was asleep when her voice came groggily out of the darkness.

"Luke...?"

"Mmm?"

"If I fall asleep...you won't leave me here in the dark, will you...?"

"No. I won't leave you."

Jenny came awake in gradual stages of awareness.

It was dark.

There was a presence with her.

But it wasn't the fearful presence of her night-mares. This was a warm, human presence. The warm, human presence of Lucas Tate.

Then she became aware of the fact that she was lying in bed with him, wearing nothing but a small pair of bikini panties.

But that simply couldn't be. She didn't do things like that.

A hazy memory came to her: she vaguely recalled Luke telling her that her gown was dirty, vaguely re-called removing the offensive garment herself.

But she didn't have time to feel any guilt or dismay because she suddenly remembered something else, something that had been locked safely away in her subconscious for weeks, something her fall down the stairs and into the darkness had released: Mexico.

Like Pandora's box opened, her black memories had come bursting out before she could slam the lid shut.

And here she was, remembering, not wanting to re-member.

Night air moved across her damp skin and a shiver ran through her. Then another.

"Jenny...?"

Luke's deep, groggy voice came to her through the darkness, touching her, comforting her. She wasn't alone. Luke was with her.

"You okay?

And like Pandora, Jenny wished she'd never opened the box, never remembered. And now that she had, she feared that the daylight hours as well as the night hours of her life would be haunted.

She wanted to tell Luke that she wasn't okay. She wanted to tell him the awful thing that had happened to her. She wanted him to put his strong arms around her and comfort her, soothe her until all the bad memories went away.

But never in her life had Jenny asked for anything from anyone, especially comfort.

Another shiver ran through her and she clamped her teeth together to keep them from chattering. "Cold . . . I'm cold . . ."

"C'mere." His warm hand touched her arm. "You're like ice."

The uncontrollable tremors kept coming, one on top of the other. "C-can't stop shaking."

He tugged at the covers, then his arm came around her, and she turned to him like a magnet to steel, letting out a gasp when her bare, cold-stiffened nipples rubbed against the coarse hairs of his chest.

Her first thought was that he didn't have any clothes on, but then she felt the button of his jeans pressing against the soft skin of her abdomen, felt the worn denim against the front of her legs. She raised her arms, skimming her hands across his biceps, circling his naked shoulders, feeling the comforting warmth of his hot skin under her cold fingertips.

"Jenny—"

His voice had quickly lost its groggy edge. Now it was tight, strained. "I forgot you weren't dressed." He tried to move away, but she clung to him.

Hold me.

"D-don't let me go. Hold me. I'm s-so cold. Just hold me till I warm up." She could feel the heat emanating from him, penetrating and soaking into her.

Gradually her shivering began to subside, slowly replaced by a pleasant, tingling warmth. But while she relaxed, while the tightness and tremors left her body, he seemed to become tenser and tenser.

What if he left? What if he simply got up and left? Panic rose in her.

Don't go.

She needed Lucas Tate. Needed to feel him close to her. Needed to be touched by him, held by him. Needed to lose herself in him so she could forget everything else.

Stay. Hold me. Make love to me.

She inched her way up, pressing her lips to his tense chest, his tense arms, his tense neck. Her lips caressed the rough sandpaper of his chin.

Make love to me. Make me forget about everything but you...

"Jenny—" He put both hands on her arms and lifted her away.

"Don't push me away!" she practically sobbed. "Please don't push me away!"

He grew very still and very quiet.

She sensed that he was thinking...waiting... listening....

His warm hands on her arms were the only two places where their bodies made contact. She could feel the damp air kissing her breasts, wishing Luke were kissing them instead. She strained toward him, feeling the stir of his breath against her parted lips.

Words tore from her, words she couldn't stop. "Stay. Make love to me." She caught her breath and held it. She could feel her racing heart, hear it thundering in her ears as she waited and waited and waited.

Then he let out a groan, like someone tortured. "Jenny." Instead of pushing her away as she feared he might, he pulled her to him, crushing his lips to hers.

She felt a small flicker of triumph before she gave up on thought and instead gave in to the feel of his mouth, the feel of his body.

He rolled her onto her back, forcing her down into the mattress with his weight, her breasts pressing full and round against his chest.

Skin against skin.

His mouth moved over hers with small, gentle tugs; then he slid his tongue between her lips and she opened them for him, feeling a chord of heat run through her.

His mouth left hers, and she mumbled a protest, not wanting him to stop touching her, ever to stop touching her....

And he didn't.

He shifted his weight so he was lying partly on his side. He cupped her breast, filling his hand, teasing the nipple with a hard thumb. When she thought she could stand it no more, his mouth, erotically wet from their deep kisses, settled over the tip of her breast, sucking, his tongue circling, circling. He moved to the other, his hair brushing slightly against her skin. As he tasted it, his hand moved down her stomach, caressing, stroking.... A finger edged the elastic band of her panties.

And stopped.

His mouth left her breast and his hand lay open and still against her taut abdomen. He was breathing hard, sounding as if he'd been running.

"Jenny—" His voice was a hard rasp. "Are you sure this time?"

"Yes. Don't stop touching me. Please don't stop touching me."

She was so afraid he would let her go, quit holding her. She wound her arms tighter, tasting the saltiness of his skin against her lips. She, who would never cling, was clinging to Lucas Tate. A frantic string of words tumbled from her of their own accord. "I don't want to think about it. Make me forget. Make it all go away."

Luke stiffened at the sudden terror-stricken panic in her voice, the underlying plea for help in her words.

"Jenny—" He leaned away, hands on her shoulders.

He was going to leave! Cold seeped into her veins, wrapped around her heart. "Don't go! Please don't go!" she begged. "Make love to me!"

Very gently, Luke put her away from him and sat up, then felt around the bed for the T-shirt he'd gotten out earlier. Finding it, he put it in her hands. "Put this on." His mind was racing, trying to think of what to say, how to handle this. He didn't want to hurt her again.

He listened to the soft sound of her pulling on the shirt, then the room was filled with silence.

Finally, she let out a pained, embarrassed laugh. "Guess this means no, huh?"

He understood just how fragile she was. Something had happened to her and whatever it was had caused her to build a wall around herself, a wall he had managed to peer over, but just for a second. "Jenny—"

"This is so embarrassing for me." Her voice was thick, sounding as if she might break into tears at any second. "So will you please leave now?"

He shifted closer, the bed dipping. "I'm staying."

"Go. I want you to go. *Please*."

He heard air being sucked into her trembling lungs as she made a last attempt at control. Then she broke down and began to sob, her whole body shaking.

What should he do? This was tearing him up. "Oh God, Jenny. Come here—"

He reached out, wrapped his arms around her shaking shoulders and pulled her against his chest.

"Go," she sobbed. "Go. I don't w-want y-you to see me l-like this."

"I'm staying. And I'm going to hold you. But we're not going to make love. Not tonight anyway."

Her hands came up and wound around his neck while she buried her face against his throat.

He talked, murmured to her over and over as if she were a child and not a woman, smoothing her hair from her brow, holding her close, rocking her.

After a while, her crying faded to jerking shudders, then sniffles, then finally stopped altogether.

"What is it you need to forget? What do you want me to make go away, Jenny?" he whispered, his lips moving against her hair. "What terrible thing has happened to you?" There was no answer, and he realized how heavily and limply she lay against him, realized she'd fallen asleep.

With the corner of the sheet, he wiped the tears from her face, then settled her back on the bed, lying down beside her.

As he lay there, it seemed that at least a thousand scenarios played across the screen of his mind as he tried to solve the mystery, to piece together what had happened to her.

Finally exhaustion must have caught up with him, too, because the next thing he knew, the overhead light was glaring down in his eyes. He winced against the brightness, having no idea what time it was, only knowing it couldn't be dawn yet; no birds were singing.

He looked at Jenny. She was sleeping deeply, still curled up next to him. A strand of hair lay across her face. Gently, so as not to wake her, he smoothed it back with one finger, feeling a stab of something close to fear when he saw the dark shadows under her eyes, saw the transparent paleness of her skin.

He reached out and turned off the bedside lamp, then carefully slid away from her, to the edge of the bed. He went over to the wall switch and had his finger on the button, ready to turn off the overhead light when a newspaper clipping on the floor caught his eye. It must have fallen out when he was rummaging through the dresser.

He picked it up. It was easy to see that the article had been read often, folded and refolded so many times that it was soft from handling.

He opened it.

In his hand was a picture of a girl's apparently lifeless body being lifted onto a stretcher. One bare, bruised arm, as thin as a child's, lay limply along her side. Even though her face was pinched and as chalky-white as the blanket that covered her, Luke knew the person in the photo was Jenny.

He stared at it for a long time, the image burning into his memory.

Then his eyes fell to the caption. And there it was— the horror Jenny had been hiding. *She'd been buried alive.*

"Sweet Jesus."

Like tumbling dominoes, everything fell into place. The dark smudges under her eyes . . . the bruise on her collarbone . . . the way she jumped at sudden noises . . . the claustrophobic fear she'd shown in the tent that day. . . . And at the stream . . . what had she said?

I don't usually sleep.

At the time, he'd thought she was confused, but now he knew differently.

There had been several times when he'd been on his way home from a late night emergency call and seen a light on in her bedroom. Children leave lights on. Jacob sometimes wanted to sleep with a light on. He said it kept the scary monsters away.

Buried alive for three days.

That wouldn't be something you just whistled away from, wouldn't be something you just forgot about. In fact, it could affect a person for the rest of her life. Might make it so she was afraid to go to sleep, afraid to turn off the lights, afraid of the dark.

His throat felt raw and swollen, his chest ached with pain for her.

His eyes dropped and he forced himself to read every word of the article. When he was done, he just stood there, stunned, heartsick and feeling more helpless than he'd ever felt in his life. The reality of what had happened to Jenny was a thousand times more horrible than his worst imaginings.

Fate had dealt her a doubly cruel blow. No wonder there were monsters in her darkness.

God! His mind struggled to comprehend what a nightmare it must have been for her, for anyone. But Jenny . . . For her to have suffered in such a way—fragile, delicate, breakable Jenny... It tore at his heart, made him angry, made him sick with grief.

No wonder he'd had the urge to protect her so many times. But it wasn't too late. Even though the blow had been dealt, the damage could be undone. It wasn't too late.

He looked over to where she lay sleeping so peacefully, like a child. How had she done it? How had she stood it? Where had she found that kind of inner strength?

Luke hadn't served in Vietnam. His number had never come up. But Danny had gone, and when he came back he was different. He wasn't the same old Danny. He sat for long periods and stared out the window; he jumped at sudden noises; he had insomnia and when he did sleep, he had nightmares. Later, his problem was given a name—post-traumatic stress disorder—but at that time it was just called shell-shock.

It had taken a lot of patience and understanding on the part of his family and friends and a Vietnam vet support group to help him through a rough time. But he'd gotten through it.

And here was Jenny, trying to fight this thing by herself. And Luke sure as hell hadn't been any help. The times he'd been around her had been spent trying to tear down any defenses she'd put up. But now that he knew, he could help her. Nobody should have to go into battle without a backup, and Luke was going to be Jenny's.

Chapter Ten

Outside, birds were singing, coaxing Jenny awake.

For a small space of time, somewhere within that mysterious realm between sleeping and waking, she wasn't consciously aware of herself as the individual named Jennifer Elizabeth May. She felt content and lazy, loved and protected. Breathing in the scent of warm, damp skin, she snuggled closer to the man beside her.

With a start, her eyes flew open and she jerked away from a snoring Lucas Tate.

Bright sunlight poured in long, latticed windows, casting checkered shadows across the polished wood floor, the bed and the sleeping man who lay sprawled facedown on the bed, weighting the mattress so she had to fight to keep from rolling back against him. She struggled to a sitting position, tugging at the tangled sheet until she was able to get it to her chin.

Unable to help herself, she stared at Luke's strong back, her eyes roaming across his muscled shoulders, following the indentation of his spine down to where it disappeared into the waistband of his faded jeans....

Then, like flickering shadows, memories of last night crept into her mind. Hazy memories of how Luke had gently washed her face and legs, how he'd carried her upstairs, how he'd held her close.

And also of the way she had clung to him, begging him to make love to her.

Oh, God.

Hot, humiliating shame ran through her. For Luke to have found her dirty and cowering in the cellar, afraid of the dark—that was unthinkable enough, but later...

The memory of her tears and her clinging and her begging made her cringe. She, who had never asked anything of anyone, had *begged*.

And the person who had witnessed her shame was here, beside her. How on earth was she going to face him when his eyes came open and he looked at her?

Night had a way of distorting things; daylight put things back in perspective. Night brought terror and weakness; with the day came shame of that weakness.

But what had happened had happened, and there was absolutely nothing to be done about it now. She only knew she couldn't bear the thought of facing Luke, having him look at her.

Run.

She almost gave in to the overwhelming urge to grab some clothes and disappear, but stopped herself.

She wouldn't run, but in her own fashion, she would hide.

She would calmly wake him and ask him to leave, pretending that last night had never happened. And if she was really lucky, he might think she'd forgotten the whole humiliating episode, which would save them both further embarrassment.

She took a deep, shaky breath, then reached out. "Luke?" she whispered.

No response.

This was entirely new to her. She'd never tried to wake a sleeping man before.

Gingerly she laid a hand upon the warm skin of his arm, shaking him once, then again.

"Luke?" Louder this time.

Eyes closed, he mumbled something about a cat and a fur ball. That disjointed statement was followed by a string of cussing. After that, he shifted to his side and folded the pillow over both ears.

She shook him again. "Luke—" Louder still.

He made a strange sound that was half groan, half growling, and she jerked her hand away.

"Get lost...beat it..." he muttered in his sleep, flopping over onto his back, rocking the bed. After settling in this new position, his hand lying limply against his bare chest, he resumed his snoring.

Jenny reached over to the bedside dresser and grabbed the alarm clock. After winding it tightly, she pulled out the plastic button and an ear-shattering clanging filled the small room.

The snoring stopped abruptly.

As the ringing dwindled to an occasional weak twang, Luke moaned and opened his eyes, looking as cross as a child awakened after a five minute nap. "What'd you do that for?" he mumbled, glowering at her through bleary eyes.

With him watching her, she was suddenly acutely aware of her puffy eyes, her burning throat, raw from tears, and the thinness of the T-shirt she was wearing.

Act as if nothing has happened, she reminded herself. *Act as if last night never occurred.*

"It's morning. You're going to have to leave."

Outside, a vehicle roared past and Jenny grabbed at the excuse it presented. "People will see your truck here," she told him hastily. "If you don't hurry, by noon the whole town will be talking about us."

Her words seemed to sink in, because he began to move, swinging his feet to the floor. Having achieved that position, he sat there on the edge of the bed, elbows on his knees, face in his hands.

"Gimme a couple of minutes to stabilize." The words came out slurred. He raked his fingers through his hair, yawned broadly and scratched his chest.

Never in her life had Jenny ever seen anyone take so long to wake up. He was like a bear coming out of hibernation.

He rubbed his head, then turned to look at her, his sun-bleached brows furrowed, his hair sticking up in every direction, his jaw dark and needing a razor.

He looked adorable.

An overwhelming feeling of tenderness rushed through her. She had seen so many sides of him, but this side, this waking up side, was entirely new. Endearing. And for some reason, she felt like crying all over again.

He bent at the waist to grope under the bed, found his boots and pulled them on. Then he stood up and tugged his shirt free of the bedpost. He shrugged his arms into the stiff fabric, buttoned it, then unselfconsciously tucked the tail into his jeans.

As if he got dressed in front of her every day.

She remained as still as a statue, scarcely daring to breathe as he leaned over her, smoothing her hair back from her brow, his fingers gentle. "Is your tetanus shot up-to-date?"

She nodded.

"Good. No sign of infection. Better leave this bandage on till tonight—then I'll be back and put on a fresh one."

She was surprised when she felt his knuckles gently stroke down her cheek. Her eyes locked with his, and what she saw there surprised her even more. Within those deep, turquoise pools was unmistakable concern.

Eyes the color of the North Atlantic gulf stream....

She must remember that. Years from now, if she stood on the deck of a ship or took a plane over the Atlantic Ocean, she could look out and say, *that* is the color of Lucas Tate's eyes.

"You going to be okay? Here by yourself?"

He'd caught her offguard. He wasn't supposed to be looking at her that way. Not with compassion and concern. It wasn't what she'd expected, not what she'd been prepared for. Her throat tightened and began to ache.

"Jenny?"

She swallowed, pressed her lips together, blinked and nodded. "Fine," she managed, dry-mouthed. "I'll be just fine."

Outside, another vehicle rolled past. Luke's eyes shifted to the window, then back to her. He smiled, splayed his hands against the mattress on either side of her and leaned close. "Jenny May, I think you've been compromised." A lazy, teasing smile—a smile she was becoming very familiar with, curved across his mouth. "You know what happens now?"

She leaned back, shoulder blades pressed against the hard wooden headboard. Like one mesmerized, she slowly shook her head.

"Guess I'll just have to salvage what's left of your tarnished reputation and marry you."

Before she could vocalize some sort of answer, before she could even think of some sort of answer to vocalize, he leaned over and pressed his lips to hers. Just when the heavy feeling was beginning to run through her, just when her eyelids started to flutter closed, he pulled away, got up and walked to the door.

Hand braced on the woodwork, he looked back. "Thanks for waking me up. I've been told that's no picnic."

Jenny was only half-aware of what he was saying. His earlier words kept echoing in her mind. It was amazing that she was able to formulate any answer at all. "You're welcome," she muttered.

"The alarm was a nice switch. Stella's favorite method is ice water in my face." He zapped her with the famous Lucas Tate smile.

Her heart fluttered.

"I'll be back before dark to look at your forehead. And talk. We have to talk." Then he turned and left, his footfalls echoing down the steps.

Long after the sounds of his departing truck had faded, Jenny remained where she was, staring at the pink flowered wallpaper.

Guess I'll just have to salvage what's left of your tarnished reputation and marry you.

He was kidding. Jenny knew that. Of course she knew that. But she couldn't help but think about the strange expression on his face, almost bemused. And his kiss...so gentle, so tender.

As a child, Jenny had learned to quit making wishes when she blew out the candles, quit putting teeth under her pillow for a tooth fairy who never came. If you don't wish, if you never expect anything, then you can't be disappointed.

But a tiny part of her couldn't help wondering what this morning with Luke had all meant. And she couldn't stop the tiny secret smile that played across her mouth.

Then she spotted the newspaper clipping on the dresser. Her smile faded and a chill touched her soul. She suddenly felt ill, dizzy. Now everything made sense. The yellowed piece of paper was lying in plain sight. Luke had read it.

He knew.

That's why he was being so nice. He pitied her.

Eyes open wide and unfocused, she picked up the pillow he'd slept on and hugged it to her, rubbing a cheek against its coolness, breathing in the scents of rain and outdoors that drifted up to her.

She didn't want his pity. Pity wasn't what she wanted from Lucas Tate.

You can blow out the candles, but don't make a wish. Never make a wish....

From downstairs, the ringing of the phone carried up to her, barely penetrating the numbness that had formed around her mind and heart.

She didn't move. She couldn't talk to anyone now.

The ringing stopped. Thirty seconds later it started again, and this time she forced herself to go downstairs to answer it.

"Jenny? How's it going up there in corn country?"

Jeffrey.

Jenny had been expecting Stella or Newt or P.J., not Jeffrey, of the chaste good-night kisses. It was jarring to hear from someone from her other life, her old life. Almost like hearing from someone from another world.

"I called last night, but there was no answer. Just checking to see if you feel well enough to come back to work yet."

She hesitated. "I've been thinking about it."

"Well, if you want to get in on a trip to Bolivia, you'll have to hurry. Our unit will be shipping out in two days. If you want, I'll put your name in and reserve a plane seat for you. What do you say? You could meet us at the Tampa airport."

A breeze drifted in the screen door, cool and damp on Jenny's bare skin. Birds chattered and corn leaves whispered to her. Jenny stood there, phone in hand, clock above the sink ticking, ticking.... At the other end of the line, Jeff was waiting to find out if she was ready to pick up the threads of her old life.

In black and white movies, the passage of time is sometimes shown with pages fluttering from a calendar. That's how her visit to Ellison seemed—as if the days and weeks had blown away before they could be fully grasped, fully appreciated.

"Jenny? You still there?"

"Yes, Jeff. I'm still here. What day did you say you'll be leaving Tampa?"

Outside, the birds were still singing, the corn leaves still calling.

Luke spent half the morning sloshing through muddy lots on John Walsh's farm while vaccinating and tattooing cattle. By ten o'clock he'd gotten his foot stepped on by a half-ton, half-crazy bull and been nailed in the shin by a flying hoof. By eleven-thirty he'd visited two more farms and performed a cesarean section on one of Slim Brockett's ewes.

Noon till two pm was reserved for office calls. During that time he juggled the treatment of small animals, phone calls, paperwork and lunch—lunch usually ending up being more wishful thinking on Luke's part than an actual event in his day. He couldn't remember when he'd last sat down and eaten an entire sandwich during the so-called lunch break.

Today he spent the time giving rabies vaccinations, setting a cat's broken leg and answering his secretary's phone while she was off shopping for a birthday present for her grandson.

In spite of the typically hectic day, his thoughts, like homing pigeons, kept flying back to one particular place, one particular person—Jenny May. He couldn't quit thinking about her, couldn't wait to be with her, talk to her. Hold her.

The end of the day finally rolled around. Luke limped home, fed the dogs, took a shower, then headed to Jenny's.

The heavy rains from last night had purified the air and lowered the temperature. The wind, as it whipped in the truck windows, was cool and fresh and smelled of grass and green clover. Luke felt his T-shirt pocket and pulled out a tongue depressor. He stuck the wooden stick in his mouth. Grape. He liked the cherry ones better, but grape was okay.

Luke wasn't sure what he would say to Jenny once he got to her house. He just knew he wanted to help her, just knew he wanted to be with her. And he knew he'd never felt like this before. Not with Cassie, not with anyone.

Back when Danny and P.J. were fresh out of high school and all geared up to get married, Luke had tried to talk some sense into his friends, telling them they were too young to be thinking about such a serious step. But Danny had insisted, said he wanted to be around P.J. all the time, said he was certain it was the right thing to do.

Now, looking back, Luke wondered if he hadn't been a little envious of them both, of that shared closeness. And now he thought maybe he understood how Danny had felt all those years ago.

Because Luke wanted to marry Jenny. He wanted to wake up beside her every morning, hold her close every night, chase away her monsters, love her.

He pulled up the gravel drive to Jenny's house, cut the engine, set the emergency brake and tossed the tongue depressor on the dash.

Then he strode up the walk and knocked on the front door. When Jenny opened it and he saw her standing there in the old-fashioned flowered dress she'd been wearing that Sunday morning at Stella's, looking soft and vulnerable, he was tempted to pull her into his arms. He needed to feel her close to him.

Then he saw the suitcase.

He stared, forgetting to breathe. His eyes darted from it to Jenny.

She nervously smoothed her hair, then crossed her arms at her waist. "I thought it was Stella at the door. She's giving me a ride to the bus station."

She hadn't expected him. She'd been hoping to get away without seeing him at all. His eyes were drawn back to that damn suitcase. He couldn't stop staring at it. "Bus station," he repeated emotionlessly.

"Yes. I'm starting a new job. My unit is being sent to Bolivia."

"Bolivia. As in South America?"

"Yes."

"Ah."

He nodded, reminding himself to breathe. The human body requires oxygen. He inhaled deeply imagining the oxygen flowing through his veins, finally reaching his brain. He wanted to grab her, tell her she couldn't leave him, that he'd been waiting for her a long time—forever it seemed.

In a sort of self-mocking dismay, he realized history was repeating itself. Maybe he was destined to watch the women he cared about walk out of his life.

There Jenny stood, suitcase packed, ready to leave dull, boring Ellison, Iowa, ready to strike out for adventure, for broader horizons.

History repeating itself. Except he didn't recall it hurting like this last time. Last time, deep down, he'd secretly felt a sense of relief. But not this time. This time it was hurting like hell.

He took a step toward her.

She backed away.

"I told you life around here would be too tame for you," he said, groping for words, not wanting her to know how much this was hurting him.

She gave an artificial laugh. Holding up one hand, she made a careful inspection of her nails. "You said I wouldn't be able to take this two-bit town very long. I guess you were right." As she spoke, she didn't look up.

He knew her brittle laughter was another of her defenses, another plate in her armor. Again he moved closer. One step. Two.

She moved back, stumbling against the carpeted steps, catching herself with her hand. Before she could get up, he pressed himself against her, knee on one step, hands on her shoulders, his face only inches from hers. Her eyes were huge as she looked up at him. He felt as though he was drowning in them.

"Tell me," he whispered, aching inside, knowing he'd lost her, realizing she'd never been his to lose. "In Bolivia—who's going to hold you at night, when it's dark, when the demons come? Who's going to hold you when the lights go out? When you dream?'' He drew in a sharp breath that stung his throat, hurt his chest. ''Who's going to make it all go away?''

''I don't know,'' she whispered huskily, desperately. ''Maybe I'll find somebody.''

Her words hung between them, causing the river of pain running through him to deepen, widen.

He swallowed, then evenly, quietly, sadly, he said, ''Maybe you will.''

Then he pushed himself away from her, got up and walked to the door. Standing in the opening, he shoved his hands deep into the front pockets of his jeans. He tilted his head back, looking up through the leaves of the ancient oak to the blue sky beyond, trying to imagine the vastness out there, sensing the overpowering size of the universe, feeling the frailty of human life.

He wanted to stop her, hold her back, keep her from going into that vastness.

But he had no claim on her. She'd said as much herself.

From a distance, he heard the sound of an approaching car.

He had thought to at least say goodbye, but his throat felt tight and suddenly he couldn't see very well, so he just walked away.

Chapter Eleven

Jenny heaved the two battered suitcases into the cavernous trunk of Stella's car, slamming the lid shut with both hands. Her eyes were drawn to the two-story farmhouse. It already looked unoccupied, abandoned, seeming to symbolize the way Jenny herself felt inside: hollow, empty, memories echoing like lonely footsteps across her mind.

Max the cat was sitting on the porch, washing his face. Earlier, Jenny had called Newt and he'd promised to stop by and feed Max, and if possible catch the kitten and take him to his house—to cat heaven, as Luke so aptly put it. A slow, sad smile touched Jenny's mouth. Then she gave the house one final look and turned away.

"I've got to stop at Talbots' and get some gas," Stella said after Jenny had settled into the passenger seat. "Ol' Bessie here really guzzles the regular." She slipped the car into gear and they headed down the sloping driveway.

On the way to Ellison, Stella was uncharacteristically quiet, almost brooding, but Jenny herself didn't feel much like talking. Instead she looked out the window, watching the sea of green cornstalks waving below a cloudless blue sky.

Before coming here, Jenny hadn't known a place like Ellison existed, except maybe in some idealistic writer's imagination. And now she was leaving, taking her night terrors and day terrors with her.

But she would also take with her a love for this place, for a little obscure town, a dot on a map. A place where people lived and dreamed, laughed and cried.

And even though Jenny was leaving, she knew life in Ellison would go on without her, never skipping a beat. She had come and would go, never causing a ripple.

When she was gone, Newt would continue to play checkers and rummy with a cat draped across his shoulders, a bottle of dandelion wine at his elbow. Mason would still roar down the back roads, terrorizing women. Stella would continue to wear her antique clothes and strange furs. Boone Bailey would collect cans and ginseng, and "all sorts of wonderful things." Little Jacob Talbot would help his godfather, Lucas Tate, make homemade strawberry ice cream.

And Lucas Tate...

Lucas Tate would still smile that special smile.

And some day he would most likely get married, most likely carry his own children on his shoulders at the county fair.

That thought hurt. Jenny didn't want to think of someone else sharing Luke's life. Someone else waking up next to him, someone else binding his cracked ribs, scolding him for being so reckless.

Someone else loving him.

The gas station bell dinged, dragging her back to now, to Stella and her gangster car with its scratchy wool upholstery that smelled of mothballs.

Instead of Danny Talbot stepping out of the cement block gas station, P.J. appeared and came around to Stella's window, leaning down to look inside. "Danny went to a Vietnam vet support group meeting in Des Moines," she told them. "So Jacob and I are running things around here. We were doing just fine till a guy showed up wanting us to patch a tire he'd taken off a grain truck." She laughed.

The station door slammed and Jacob came dashing out, looking adorable in faded bib overalls, a white T-shirt and a green cap just like the one his father had been wearing the day of the fair.

While P.J. pumped gas, Jacob came and stood on the running board, hanging on Jenny's door frame so he could thrust two wilted dandelions at her. "Here's a flower for you and one for Mrs. Tate."

"Why, thank you." Jenny took them, handing one to Stella.

"They're closed now," Jacob informed her, "but if you take them home and put them in water, they'll open back up in the morning."

"I'm not going home," Jenny had to tell him. "I'm on my way to the bus station right now."

"Then I guess yours won't open back up."

Jenny stuck the flower in a buttonhole of her dress. "I like it this way too."

"You never got to have any homemade ice cream. Mom was gonna ask you to come to our house for some."

Jenny tried to smile at little Jacob, but feared she wasn't doing a very good job of it. She felt more like crying. "That would have been nice."

"Come on, Jacob." P.J. put her hand on his shoulder. "They have to go. Jenny has a bus to catch."

"Bye." Jenny waved.

P.J. and Jacob lifted a hand in return.

Jenny's last glimpse of Ellison would be forever etched in her mind: the image of mother and son standing side by side in front of the flat-roofed station with its peeling paint, P.J. with her long, straight blond hair blowing in the breeze, Jacob in his overalls, clutching a straggly fistful of yellow dandelions, the picture framed by shimmering fields of green corn.

At the tiny bus station, they unloaded the luggage and Jenny purchased her ticket at the outside window. "You don't have to wait with me," Jenny told

Stella since there was no waiting area inside the station. The bus is due in ten minutes."

"But I want to wait, dear." Stella fumbled with the clasp on her purse. "I wouldn't think of leaving until you're safely on the bus." Her voice cracked on the last word. Then, to Jenny's horror, Stella burst into a torrent of dramatic weeping.

"Oh, Jenny. I am sorry." She looped the double straps of her purse over one arm and finally managed to locate a Kleenex. "It's just that you're breaking my poor Lucas's heart." She sniffled. "And the whole thing is my fault. That's what I get for being a meddling old woman."

"Breaking his heart?" Where had Stella come by such a ridiculous notion? "Stella, you're wrong."

Jenny would have given anything to be able to believe Stella's words, but she knew better. The strongest emotion Lucas Tate felt for her was pity.

With the fingers of both hands, Stella smoothed the wrinkles from the tissue she held. "No, I know Luke. He cares about you." She gave her nose a loud blow. "He loves you. And I'm afraid of what this will do to him—jilted twice in a lifetime."

"Jilted! I'm not jilting him. We aren't engaged. We never even dated."

"Doesn't matter. I know the signs. He's started smoking again. He denies it, but I have a nose like a hound and I've smelled smoke on his clothes."

"Smoking? Smoking and falling in love are two completely different things. One has nothing to do with the other."

"Oh, yes they do. He hadn't touched a cigarette for almost four months now. I was so proud of him. Why would he start again after almost four months?"

"Stress from his job? I don't know. Oh, Stella, Luke doesn't love me. He feels sorry for me. That's all."

"So? Luke feels sorry for everyone and everything. Most softhearted, hardheaded man I know."

Jenny heard the deep rumble of an engine, then the loud whoosh of diesel brakes. A bus pulled in, the sign on top reading CHICAGO.

She looked back at her friend. "Don't cry—please."

Jenny was dangerously close to tears herself. What was she going to do? She hated to abandon Stella like this.

She glanced over her shoulder. The bus driver was tossing her suitcases into the storage compartment. The door slammed shut. "All set."

She turned back to the older woman, giving her a hug. "Stella, I have to go. Thank you for all you've done for me. I'll write. And you're wrong about Luke."

Stella shook her head and smiled sadly. "No, no I'm not. Think about it. You just think about it, honey."

Jenny turned and headed toward the bus. With each dragging step came an increasing, uneasy doubt. What if Stella was right? What if she wasn't just match-making... meddling...?

If so, then Jenny was making a terrible mistake, allowing something very precious to slip through her fingers.

Luke grabbed the cigarettes off the counter and stuck them in the breast pocket of his T-shirt. Then he tucked the half finished six-pack under his arm. Equipped with everything a bachelor could possibly need, he headed out the kitchen door to the barn.

Shoving a shoulder against the hanging door, he rolled it all the way open and slipped inside the cool, dim refuge.

Bales of hay were stacked against the far wall. The barn smelled of seasons past, decades and generations gone. Loose alfalfa stirred under his boot heels, dredging up more recent memories of hot summer days spent sweating on the back of a hayrack.

Close to the land... A man's gotta live close to the land in order to keep his perspective.

Luke didn't use the barn much anymore. At lambing time he kept the few sheep he owned inside. The rest of the time he just used it for hay storage. It hadn't changed all that much over the years. Back when he and Danny were in high school, they used to come here to drink and smoke. And here he was, drinking and smoking.

Another case of history repeating itself.

He thought about climbing into the hayloft, but it seemed like too much of an effort so he just sprawled out on the floor, back against a hay bale, stretching his legs in front of him, crossing them at the ankles. He twisted a beer free of a plastic loop, popped the top and took a long drink.

The barn door faced west, and from where he was, Luke could see that the sun had sunk low enough for its evening glow to spill inside. The scattered orange light reached him across the hay-strewn floor, its splintered shafts making him think of the religious paintings that still hung in the Bible school rooms at the old Ellison Church. Outside, the ancient windmill creaked and groaned, the blades barely turning.

In another hour, it would be dark. And Jenny would be out there somewhere, in that darkness.

It was going to take some time for him to get used to the idea of her being gone. Kind of like when someone close to you dies. There are those flickering fragments of time when you forget they're gone and for that brief millisecond you are able to put your grief aside and give undivided attention to something else, and then it happens—that's when it hits you, when you think you see them or hear them. Then you remember again, and the loss sweeps over you, more painful than before.

That's how it was going to be for him.

Luke was getting ready to take another drink of beer when the light bathing the inside of the barn was cut off.

Standing silhouetted in the warm glow of the setting sun was Jenny May.

Chapter Twelve

Jenny's position at the barn door afforded her an unhindered view of Luke. He was sitting on the hay-littered floor, his back against a bale, looking real and strong and devastatingly handsome in his faded jeans and the yellow Humane Society T-shirt that stretched tightly across his chest and biceps. He was staring up at her, one arm draped over a bent knee, beer can dangling from his limp hand.

He took a long drink, brought his hand back down and refixed his stare on her. "Miss your bus? Or did you come to take one last gander at the two-bit vet before you leave the two-bit town?"

"Are you drunk?" she asked suspiciously.

"I'm working on it, but so far all I've achieved is a

pleasant buzz." He held up what was left of a six pack—two cans. "Wanna beer?"

Jenny wasn't crazy about beer, but she nodded, his unconcerned attitude reminding her of the first time they'd met, when he'd barged into her house and plopped down in front of the television to watch *Green Acres*.

With a booted foot, he shoved a hay bale in her direction. "Have a seat." He wiped bits of clinging chaff from a sweating beer can, popped the top and handed it to her as she sat down.

The beer was cold and mellow, better tasting than she remembered beer to be.

Luke leaned back and looked around him. "Yeah, sitting in this old barn stirs up a lot of memories. When we were kids, Danny and I used it for a clubhouse. Later we graduated to girls and barn dances. One Halloween we even used it for a haunted house." He pointed above his head. "I was Dracula and swooped down from that pulley up there. Scared the beejeebies out of Luetta Smith."

Jenny could almost picture it. "What nice memories," she said a little wistfully, maybe a little enviously, wishing she'd been there, wishing she'd been the girl he'd asked to the dance.

"You mean boring memories, don't you?"

"No, I mean nice."

She knew he was referring to what she'd said earlier, about Ellison being a dull, two-bit town. She was about to tell him she hadn't meant it when she felt his hand on her bare ankle. A thrill ran through her and she completely forgot what she was going to say. When she looked down at him, their eyes met and locked.

"Jenny May," he said quietly, huskily from his position on the floor near her hip, "what are you doing here?"

Say it, she told herself. Tell him why you came. *Tell him you love him.*

But the intense way he was looking up at her made her heart knock against her rib cage, made her nerves quake, her courage falter. She had so much to lose— everything to lose.

"My cut," she whispered, dry-mouthed. "I forgot to have you look at my cut."

He let go of her ankle and his eyes widened with what she could only interpret as incredulity. "Your cut?" He twisted the beer can down into the hay near his leg.

His reaction told her everything. Suddenly she knew she'd been wrong, that Stella had been been wrong, and that she had just lost it all.

She didn't understand how her heart could still beat, how her chest could still rise and fall with each painful breath, because it seemed as if she had died.

Her pride was her only salvation. She wouldn't allow herself to fall apart in front of him. She had done that before—never again.

She tried to withdraw mentally, to put some distance between herself and her emotions. The talent had served her so well in the past, but this time it didn't work. The door refused to be closed, the wall would not go up, her suit of armor was nowhere to be found, leaving her raw and exposed and full of a new kind of pain.

She waved a hand in an airy gesture she'd often seen her mother use. "Never mind. I'm sorry I interrupted your—your private party or whatever—" Blindly she thrust her beer at him, leaped to her feet and ran, her cotton dress whirling around her knees.

Run. Hide.

She was almost at the end of the driveway when she heard footfalls crunching on the gravel behind her.

"Jenny! Where are you going? Jenny!"

She kept running.

Strong, warm fingers wrapped around her bare arm, stopping her, pulling her around to stare at the front of a yellow T-shirt. She remembered it from the fair, but she didn't remember the letters being blurry.

Animals Are Kind to Dumb People. She blinked and the letters became more defined.

"Jenny, wait." He stopped, catching his breath.

She deliberately kept her gaze focused on the lettering of his shirt. A finger touched her chin, ever so lightly, slowly tilting her face up until she was forced to meet his gaze, finding that it wasn't mocking as she had feared. Strangely enough, his expression was tender, maybe even a little wistful.

"Come back inside and I'll check your cut," he coaxed. "Come on."

His voice was so warm, his smile so bittersweet that there was no way Jenny could refuse him. No way on earth.

Once inside, he gently pushed her down on a hay bale. "Wait here. I'll be right back." When he got to the barn door, he turned. "You won't run off, will you?"

She shook her head. "No."

He flashed her a smile, then disappeared.

When he returned, he was carrying a small plastic box and a brown bottle of hydrogen peroxide. With one hand, he dragged a hay bale next to hers and straddled it to sit facing her, his leg pressed against her knee. She could feel the warmth radiating from him, smell the scent of outdoors coming from his clothes, his skin.

Her eyelids fluttered shut. Sitting very still, she let herself absorb his presence, hardly daring to breathe.

She heard the sound of tearing paper, then of a bottle cap being unscrewed. Fingertips lightly stroked her hair back from her brow, then carefully eased the bandage away. "This might sting a bit."

Cold, wet cotton touched her forehead.

When he was done, he covered the cut with another bandage, carefully smoothing it down. There were sounds of things being put away. Then silence.

Jenny opened her eyes to stare directly into twin pools of fathomless blue. Eyes the color of the ocean.

Her heart constricted, her breath caught.

His gaze flickered from her eyes to her lips, then back to her eyes. "Is there anything else I can do for you?" he whispered huskily.

Seize the Moment.

She'd read that on a poster somewhere.

"A kiss," she said with a great show of outward calm. She moved closer. "A kiss would be nice."

One side of his mouth turned up, and she could see the humor reaching out to her from the warm depths of his eyes. "As a general rule, I don't kiss my patients—but I'll be more than happy to make an exception this time."

He moved slowly, as if afraid to break the mood, as if afraid of startling her. His arms encircled her and then he was pulling her close. One hand came up to support the back of her head, his fingers threading through her hair all the way to her scalp. His breath caressed the side of her face . . . her mouth.

Her eyelids drifted closed.

Then she felt the warmth of his lips pressing against hers. Her hands slid up his muscular arms, across the softness of his T-shirt. She could feel his heartbeat against her chest.

Blood rushed through her veins, swift and fast. She felt alive. This was exactly where she should be, where she belonged. With Luke everything was clear, focused, right—so that when he pulled away she felt abandoned, lost, confused.

"Jenny, I have to know why you *really* came back."

Beneath his breathless rush of words, she thought she detected a hint of desperation. Reawakened hope became a small flickering flame within her soul. Maybe, just maybe she hadn't lost after all.

She had to know. She couldn't leave if there was a chance that her cared, really cared. "I couldn't leave without finding out if you feel the way I feel," she told him.

"And how do you feel?"

She pulled in a trembling breath. "I want to be with you." She stopped, unable to bring herself to say more. Not yet. And maybe she'd said too much already.

She became aware of his stillness. Then he let go of her completely, pushed himself to his feet and moved away to stand silently just inside the barn door, one hand braced high on the frame.

Watching him, suddenly she could sense his vulnerability, feel the weight of his sadness.

The layered years of Jenny's invisible protective shell fell away. Going on instinct, she came and stood beside him. Dew was settling on the grass, cicadas whirred among the rustling corn leaves, birds called, the windmill creaked.

"When I was a kid," Luke said, his gaze directed outward to where a huge, fiery sun touched the yellow tassels shimmering like gold atop the fields of corn, "the vet for this area was a guy who should have retired twenty years before he did, but nobody else was interested in starting a practice here. Doc Kiley's remedy for almost everything was oil of turpentine—usually painted along the animal's spine with a camel hair brush. Needless to say, the pet cemetery got a lot of business. When I was twelve, I made up my mind to become a vet and practice here in Ellison. It took a while to get some of the old-timers off the turpentine and sold on new methods, but most of them finally came around.''

Luke fell silent. The windmill groaned, as if waiting.

''I could never leave here. Too many people depend on me.'' His words had a ring of finality to them, like the last line of a tragic play.

Did Luke think she would want to leave Ellison, just as Cassie had? Her earlier taunt came back to her, and the flicker of hope grew, became a small steady flame.

Make a wish. Blow out the candles.

She squeezed her eyes shut. Then she did something she hadn't done for years, not since very early childhood when fairies still slept in curled leaves and a man still lived in the moon, before her eyes had become clouded by harsh realities.

Jenny made a wish.

And it wasn't a small wish. She wished for the love of Lucas Tate.

''Before I came here,'' she said, opening her eyes, ''I didn't know places like this actually existed. I thought county fairs and ice cream socials were cherished memories of the past. Then I came to Ellison and was completely swept off my feet. I fell in love with the countryside, with the town, with the people—'' She paused, swallowing. ''Especially one person.''

Luke turned to look at her, the glow left by the setting sun reflecting in his eyes, his expression guarded. ''What are you saying, Jenny?''

"I'm saying I want you to be the one to hold me when the demons come, when the lights go out—when I dream." Her voice dropped to a husky whisper. "I want you to be the one to hold me and make it all go away, because I love you."

Seconds went by.

Her life was ticking away, and he was silent.

"Oh, Lord, Jenny May."

Then he caught her to him, enfolding her in his strong arms, rocking her against his chest. "You've just made me the happiest man in the county, in the universe."

He held her that way for a long time. Then he tilted her chin up. "I love you, Jenny." Her mouth opened under his and he kissed her deeply, pulling her body compactly against his.

"Let's really give the town something to gossip about," Luke whispered against her hair. "Let's get married as soon as we can get a license."

"Let's," she agreed wholeheartedly. His fingers were drawing small circles at the nape of her neck, making her feel limp and warm all over.

Something crunched in his shirt pocket. He drew back, pulled out a flattened pack of cigarettes and tossed them over his shoulder. "I won't be needing those anymore."

Then he took both her hands and urged her back into the barn, pulling her down beside him in a pile of soft hay, the crushed scent of clover stirring up sweet memories of days gone by, but even sweeter promises of tomorrow.

Then he was kissing her again, his lips moving down her neck. In between the kisses, he talked. And if his words were somewhat breathless, Jenny liked it all the more. "Boone Bailey used to be some kind of fly-by-night minister," he said. "He'll probably want to officiate. Afterward, we can make it legal at the courthouse."

He kissed her again.

"And Stella will want to be there to take credit for everything. And she'll probably wear her fur in honor of the occasion," he warned.

"It wouldn't seem right if she didn't." A gasp escaped Jenny when his lips pressed against the hollow of her throat.

It was getting terribly hard to focus her thoughts with his hands and mouth moving over her the way they were. He kissed her some more, then stopped. "Ah, sweet Jenny. I can't keep my hands off you— I'm sorry."

"I like your hands on me."

"You do?"

"Yes." She had her head against his chest, listening to his heartbeat. "And your mouth. I like your mouth on me, too." His heartbeat quickened, then she heard his breathless laugh and he pulled her even closer.

Suddenly she noticed that while they'd been lying together, darkness had fallen. "It's dark," she said, surprised to find that nighttime, something she had feared and dreaded for so long, had come unnoticed.

"Do you want to go inside?"

"Let's stay here. I'm not afraid as long as you're with me."

"Then I'll be sure to stay with you." He was all set to kiss her again, when through the barn door a trailing brightness moved across the sky to disappear over the silhouetted horizon. "A falling star," Luke whispered against Jenny's smooth temple. "Better make a wish."

"I already made one earlier."

"Make another."

"I have everything I want."

"Then I'll make one."

He wished. "Do you want to know what I wished for?"

"Don't tell me. It won't come true if you tell me."

Luke smiled, loving her.

And as he held Jenny close, feeling her soft warmth, her head resting against his heart, he thought about how lucky he was. He would take care of her, help her get over her trauma and her nightmares. It would take time, but he could afford to be patient. Because that special place in his heart—the place that had been empty for a long, long time—was now filled. Together they would stay in Ellison, together they would hang on to some of the old ways, the good ways, the magic.

It would happen because he had wished it, and because Luke had never quite outgrown believing in magic.

* * * * *

FOUR UNIQUE SERIES FOR EVERY WOMAN YOU ARE ...

Silhouette Romance

Love, at its most tender, provocative, emotional ... in stories that will make you laugh and cry while bringing you the magic of falling in love.

6 titles per month

Silhouette Special Edition

Sophisticated, substantial and packed with emotion, these powerful novels of life and love will capture your imagination and steal your heart.

6 titles per month

Silhouette Desire

Open the door to romance and passion. Humorous, emotional, compelling—yet always a believable and sensuous story—Silhouette Desire never fails to deliver on the promise of love.

6 titles per month

Silhouette Intimate Moments

Enter a world of excitement, of romance heightened by suspense, adventure and the passions every woman dreams of. Let us sweep you away.

4 titles per month

Silhouette Romance®

COMING NEXT MONTH

AVAILABLE THIS MONTH